*Sterling runs away—again!*

"She's going to jump the fence!" Melanie cried.

Christina heard that and realized Sterling was heading for the outside line again, at a dead run. Sterling's mane whipped her face and hoofbeats pounded in her ears. As the ground rushed by underneath her, all Christina could do was wait for the fall.

An instant later she felt Sterling heave herself into the air, and caught a glimpse of the green vertical underneath her as the horse jumped the fence. Christina was thrown over the horse's right side. She had a curious, tumbling view of the mare's belly and hind legs cantering over her while she waited for the impact. She had just a split second to be mildly amazed that she hadn't been stepped on before she felt all the air rush out of her lungs as she met the ground in a bone-jarring thud.

THOROUGHBRED

# STERLING'S SECOND CHANCE

CREATED BY
JOANNA CAMPBELL

WRITTEN BY
ALLISON ESTES

HarperPaperbacks
*A Division of* HarperCollins*Publishers*

HarperPaperbacks
*A Division of* HarperCollins*Publishers*
10 East 53rd Street, New York, N.Y. 10022-5299

---







ISBN 0-06-106799-7



First printing: May 1998

Printed in the United States of America



❖ 10 9 8 7 6 5 4 3 2 1

*Especially for my niece,*
*Cassidy Nicole Smith*

"JUMP THAT OUTSIDE LINE AGAIN, CHRISTINA, BUT THIS time put six strides between the fences instead of five. Then come around and jump the liverpool."

Christina Reese gave her riding instructor, Mona Gardener, a nod that meant she understood. She tucked a stray lock of her strawberry blond hair behind her ear. Then she shortened her reins and urged her four-year-old Thoroughbred mare into a trot. "Did you hear that, Sterling?" Christina said to the horse. "You've got to slow down and listen to me."

Sterling Dream tossed her head and let out a snort. Her dapple gray coat was darkened with sweat even though it was early morning and still fairly cool. The summer sun glinted on the mare's muscled haunches as she cantered, and flashed in the silver streaks of her black mane and tail.

"That's it," Mona said, nodding approvingly as Christina moved Sterling out of the circle and headed toward the two jumps. Tall, slim Mona stood still near the center of the arena, her hands on her hips. Her head turned slightly as she watched Christina canter by. Christina could feel Mona's clear gray eyes taking in every detail of her form as she rode. "That's your pace," Mona encouraged. "Now just hold her there. Don't let her speed up."

Christina pushed her heels down and lifted her chin, trying to seem confident to Mona and to her horse, but inside she didn't feel very confident at all.

"Easy, girl," she murmured to the horse as she came closer and closer to the first jump. Sterling had been coming along beautifully ever since Christina had gotten her in a claiming race at Belmont Park racetrack in the spring. With Mona's guidance, they'd been training for a two-day event coming up at a neighboring farm called Foxwood Acres. The event included a novice horse trial on the first day for teams of horses and riders who were just starting out in combined training. The three riders on each team would be individually tested in dressage and on a cross-country jump course. Then their scores would be combined for the overall team score.

Christina wasn't worried about the dressage test. She and Sterling had been practicing the training-level test for weeks. Christina knew the moves by heart, and she thought by now Sterling must know them, too, because the mare seemed to know what cue Christina was going to give her even before she gave it. It was the jumping that Christina was worried about.

She had always thought jumping was the best thing about riding, and it had always been easy for her. She was as comfortable jumping a horse over a three-foot fence as she was asleep in her own bed. Just when she'd been ready to move on to jumping higher fences, she'd found Sterling.

At first Sterling had seemed to love jumping as much as Christina. But lately the mare had been rushing the fences. And during the past week she had even run out a couple of times, ducking to the side at the last second instead of jumping. Christina had nearly fallen off both times because she hadn't expected it. She glanced over at the liverpool, a four-foot-wide rectangle of water with a low rail set across the middle of it to encourage the horse to clear it. In the cross-country course at Foxwood there was a water ditch. Christina had been trying to practice jumping the liverpool to get Sterling ready for it. But now she was having trouble with plain old verticals, and so far she hadn't even gotten Sterling to go near the water. With the event so close, Christina was beginning to really worry. Why had Sterling suddenly become difficult over fences?

With a final hopeful glance at Mona, Christina found herself facing the first jump, a vertical made of two rails painted green. The jump was only two and a half feet high. Christina had been schooling over jumps a foot higher, so it should have been easy for her. But the two-and-a-half-foot fence seemed to loom as high as a four-foot oxer. Christina could feel butterflies stir in her stomach with every stride as they cantered toward the jump.

"That's it, that's it," Mona said encouragingly. "Now just be consistent, Chris. If you stay exactly the same, she'll stay the same."

Christina heard Mona's words, but her eyes were fixed over the top rail of the fence. From long experience she bent forward into two-point position, ready to jump, and prepared herself to feel the thrust as Sterling launched her powerful body into the air to clear the fence.

She should have felt the wonderful, soaring sensation as the horse pushed off with her hindquarters and became airborne in a soundless moment of perfect flight. She should have felt the momentary pressure in her legs and heels as she held herself steady on the landing after the jump, and then, like clockwork, the rhythmic canter away as she headed for the next jump.

But what Christina felt instead was the unpleasant sensation of being thrown forward over her horse's right shoulder as the mare stopped and ducked to the left to avoid jumping the fence. Christina found herself almost lying on Sterling's neck, hanging on with all her might as she struggled to get herself centered over the horse again. She would have fallen off, except that she had yanked on one of the reins as she pitched forward. Sterling's head had shot up in protest, but it had also kept Christina from going completely over and off.

"Pick your head up, Chris, and settle yourself back into the saddle." Out of habit, Christina obeyed Mona's calm command, and though she hadn't thought she could move, she did manage to push herself back and find the saddle again.

Sterling had been trotting swiftly toward the gate that led out of the arena. She stopped when she reached it and looked around expectantly, as if she thought someone should appear and open it for her. Mona laughed.

"Well, Princess, sorry your attendants aren't here to open the palace gates for you," she joked as she walked over to Sterling and put a hand on the reins.

Ordinarily Christina would have laughed, too. Mona was her mother's best friend, and Christina had been taking lessons from her since she was four years old. One of the best things about Mona's teaching was that she was good at getting students to laugh at their mistakes. Mona never yelled, the way Christina had seen some instructors yell at their students; she was the best riding instructor in the world, as far as Christina was concerned. She was also one of the best event riders Christina had ever seen. Twice Mona had qualified to be an alternate on the three-day event team for the Olympics. Ever since she was little, Christina could remember wanting to be as great a rider as Mona.

But right then Christina forgot all that. She was angry—angry at Sterling for running out at the jump, angry at Mona for joking about it, and most of all angry at herself for not being able to get Sterling over a little vertical without almost falling off. She hadn't even made it to the liverpool, which was the most difficult of the three fences. She stared fiercely at Sterling's withers while she impatiently stabbed at the stirrups with her feet, and she grew angrier still as she kept missing the left one.

Mona was holding Sterling's reins to steady the horse while Christina got herself together. She watched Christina trying to find the stirrup, and finally she held it steady in front of her foot. "Hey, what's the matter? You okay, Chris?" Mona was looking at Christina with concern.

"It's not funny!" Christina snapped. "Why are you laughing at me?"

Mona cocked her head, her eyes narrowing as she scrutinized Christina. "I'm not laughing at you," she said quietly. "You know that. Why are you so upset?"

"I'm not upset," Christina said through clenched teeth. She shortened the reins and turned Sterling away from the gate. The mare had been standing relaxed, but now her head went up again and her ears began to flick forward and back nervously. Christina felt the horse break into an antsy jog, and she shortened the reins more and pulled impatiently on them. Sterling walked, but Christina could feel that the mare wanted to move out. She gripped the reins hard with her hands, both to hold the mare at a walk and to keep her hands from trembling.

"Well, then, are you ready to try it again?" Mona asked.

Christina nodded. She wasn't ready at all. But she knew she had to make Sterling jump the fence. She understood that she couldn't put the horse away until she got her going nicely again; otherwise Sterling would think it was okay to run out at the fences.

"Wait a second, Chris."

She had been about to start her trot circle again when Mona stopped her. Impatiently Christina pulled on the reins. Sterling stopped for a second, then reacted to Christina's tension by pulling with her head and trying to step forward again. Christina leaned back and seesawed on the reins, the way she'd sometimes had to do in order to stop the hard-mouthed pony she used to ride.

But Sterling's mouth was soft. The mare's head shot up, then she lifted her front legs and reared in protest at the pain she felt. Christina had dealt with all kinds of bucking, bolting, and craziness from her pony, but Sterling's rearing alarmed her. What if the horse fell backward on top of her? "Mona!" she cried. "What's the matter with her?"

"Release the reins and lean forward," Mona commanded.

Christina pushed her hands forward and leaned toward the horse's neck. As soon as she did, Sterling put her front feet on the ground again.

Christina was still crouched over the horse's neck. Sterling snorted uneasily and stamped her foot but stood still.

"Why's she doing that? What's the matter with her?" Christina asked, feeling her voice tremble with the tears of frustration that were threatening to come.

Mona shook her head. "Chris, she's sensitive, you know that. Sterling's reacting to your tension. You've got to relax and just finesse her a little more. A horse like this gives you a completely different kind of ride than your pony."

"But I didn't do anything!" Christina protested. "I just want her to stop and listen to me, and she keeps trying to go, go, go!"

"Sterling's a Thoroughbred," Mona reminded her. "If you pull on her, she wants to run. You've got to stop using the reins so much and tell her more with your body language when you want her to slow down."

"But I don't understand why she's behaving like this all of a sudden," Christina protested. "She's been so perfect up until the last week or so."

Mona sighed. "It's pretty normal, Christina. Sterling's been recovering from her life as a racehorse and getting used to her new surroundings. She's starting to relax and feel at home here, but her personality is also showing more. She's going to test you a little more, now that she's feeling sure of herself, and how you respond to it is going to make all the difference in her behavior."

"What do you mean?" Christina asked.

"I mean you've got to react calmly and discipline Sterling consistently if you want her to keep improving. I never saw you worry about anything Trib did when you rode him," Mona pointed out.

Trib, whose real name was Tribulation, was the pony Christina had ridden and shown before she outgrew him and got Sterling. It was true that he'd behaved as badly as a pony could, and it had never bothered Christina for an instant. She tried to think what the difference was but couldn't. "It just wasn't the same with Trib," Christina said.

Mona seemed to know what she was thinking. "Chris, you didn't have any expectations with Trib. You knew he was rotten from the start, so you just made up your mind that you and he were going to get better together, no matter what. And that's exactly what happened."

Christina nodded. She and Trib had ended up winning many championships together when he finally began to shape up. But no matter how perfectly he was behaving, Christina had always been on guard for a buck or a spook. So it never rattled her when it happened, and she almost always stayed on.

Mona went on. "Sterling started off behaving nicely, but now she's testing you a little. You can't be surprised by that. She's a young, sensitive, intelligent horse who's been through an awful lot in her four years. I know how much you dreamed of owning a horse, but you can't expect Sterling to be perfect just because you imagined it that way."

Christina nodded again and reached out to stroke Sterling's sweaty neck. "You're right," she mumbled. "I'm sorry, Sterling. I'll try to be more patient with you." It was as easy as that. She would try not to feel so tense about the jumps, and Sterling would relax along with her. Then she'd start jumping perfectly again. Christina was sure of it.

"Good girl," Mona said approvingly. "I know you can do it."

"Hi, Christina! Hi, Mona!"

Christina glanced up and saw her best friend, Katie Garrity, walking toward the arena. She was with three other kids. One was Christina's twelve-year-old cousin, Melanie Graham, who was spending the summer with Christina and her parents. Another was Dylan Becker, a boy Christina knew from school and from the barn. Katie and Dylan were the other two members of Christina's team for the upcoming horse trial at Foxwood. Christina had become friends with Dylan that spring. He waved at her, and instantly her heart took a couple of extra thuds as she felt the weird jumble of emotion she always experienced around Dylan. It confused her, as usual, so she gave him a quick wave and then tried to figure out who the fourth girl was—she was tall and blond, and even from a distance Christina could tell she was wearing perfectly fitted riding breeches and boots, while the rest of the kids wore jeans and chaps with battered paddock boots or riding sneakers.

But she didn't have much time to wonder who the girl was, because Mona was saying something to her and handing her a crop.

". . . so if she runs out again, give her one good smack with it. She's smart enough that if she gets in trouble for it once, you probably won't have to get after her again." Mona was giving the instructions in the same calm, confident voice she always used, but she might as well have been speaking an alien tongue to Christina.

Christina was looking at Mona and the crop incredulously. "You want me to hit her?" Christina asked. "How can I hit her after what she went through at the track?"

"Sterling was *abused* by her groom, Christina," Mona said. "The man was ignorant and afraid, and he hit her on the neck and head with a chunk of wood. That is completely different from educating your horse to respect your leg by giving her a little swat with a riding crop. You use the crop to teach your horse to obey your leg and move forward when you ask; that is *not* the same thing as abuse."

Christina felt her eyes blur with tears as she remembered how she'd seen Sterling abused at Belmont before she'd managed to convince everyone what was happening. Now all that was behind her, of course, but the horse was still sensitive about certain people handling her, especially men. And Christina hadn't carried a crop with Sterling since she'd gotten her. She wasn't at all sure she was ready to start now.

"I don't need the crop," Christina said. "I can get her over without it. I wasn't expecting her to run out. It was my fault. I'll just keep a lot of left leg on her; she'll go over it." Christina gathered up her reins and looked toward the two jumps on the outside line.

"Christina, take the crop," Mona said. "She's gotten away with running out too many times now. You wouldn't hit her for it last week when she did it, and now she's started it again. If you don't discipline her for it, she's only going to get worse."

Christina had always followed Mona's advice and had never once doubted her. Mona was looking intently at her, waiting for her to concede.

Christina stared at the crop Mona held out to her. She had always carried a crop or a bat with her pony, and she had used it on him plenty of times. But the more she thought about the crop in Mona's hand, the more she knew she couldn't possibly use it on

Sterling. Slowly Christina shook her head. "I'll make her do it without the crop," she said firmly. Before Mona could argue, she turned Sterling and trotted toward the fence rail.

As she reached the rail, Christina noticed her cousin, along with Katie, Dylan, and the other girl, standing together near the gate. As Sterling cantered by them, Christina heard the blond girl laugh. Christina glanced over her shoulder and caught the girl's eye for a second. She couldn't be sure, but it seemed to her that the girl was laughing at her. Christina felt her face turn hot and red, but she tried to ignore it. She had a job to do.

She came off the turn and cantered straight toward the green vertical. As each stride brought her closer to the jump, she pressed more firmly with her left leg. She was determined not to let Sterling run out this time. *Three, two, one,* she counted to herself, and then she was at the takeoff spot. She gave Sterling an extra bump with her left leg and felt the mare surge off the ground and clear the fence.

At the same time Christina allowed herself a satisfied smile. She had been right. She hadn't needed the crop. She knew her own horse, didn't she? For a split second she glanced at Mona and saw her face unchanged as she watched Christina canter down the line toward the second fence.

After three strides Christina realized she was more than halfway down the line, and Mona had said to do it in six. She knew she'd better slow Sterling or she was going to put five quick strides in again. Christina sat up a little and, keeping the pressure from her leg steady, closed her fingers on the reins to collect the horse.

Christina felt Sterling obey. She slowed her canter in time and put in three more strides before the fence instead of two. With a glance toward the liverpool, her next jump, Christina relaxed and bent forward into two-point position at the takeoff spot. She had ridden the line perfectly and she knew it. She hoped Dylan was watching.

The next thing she knew, she was lying flat on her back at the bottom of the jump. Sterling had ducked her right shoulder and spun to the left to avoid jumping the fence. Christina hadn't even had time to react.

She lay still for a moment, trying to decide if she was hurt. But it had happened too fast for her to tense up. She was fine, she knew. She jumped up quickly and looked around for Sterling. Suddenly she remembered the other kids, and she hoped Dylan *hadn't* been watching. But when she turned her head she saw that he was halfway across the ring already, hurrying toward her.

"Oh, no," Christina said miserably.

Mona had already reached her side. "Are you all right?" she asked, gazing into Christina's hazel eyes.

"I'm fine," Christina said, a little too loudly. But

she was shaking, and she thought for a second she might throw up.

Dylan had almost reached them, but when he saw that Christina was on her feet, he stopped a few yards away. Christina was distracted by the concerned expression in his brown eyes. Was he worried about her? The thought stirred the butterflies from the bottom of her stomach all the way up into her chest.

Katie and Melanie were hurrying right behind him. "Omigosh, Chris, are you okay?" Katie asked. Her blue eyes were huge with concern under her ash-blond bangs.

"She's white as a ghost," Melanie said dramatically. "Maybe she's going to pass out."

Melanie sounded hopeful when she said that. Christina wasn't too shaken to give her cousin a sharp look.

"She's fine," Mona assured them. "Let's not crowd her. Can one of you catch Sterling, please?"

"Cassidy's got her," Melanie said, gesturing across the ring.

Christina looked for her horse and saw the blond girl, Cassidy Smith, leading Sterling toward them. There was an air of casual confidence about the girl, as if she had seen all this before and was used to it. Christina had the distinct impression that Cassidy had always been the one who caught the horse and never the one who fell off.

Christina noticed that Dylan wasn't looking at her

anymore. He was looking at Cassidy with an expression that Christina took for admiration. She didn't like the feeling it gave her. She also didn't like seeing Cassidy hold her horse.

"I've got her, thanks," Christina said, stepping toward Cassidy and taking her horse's reins. But when she moved forward, she was surprised to find that she was unsteady, pins and needles shooting through her arms and legs.

"Whoa there," Mona said, putting an arm around her. "You landed pretty hard, and the back of your helmet is dirty. You may have bumped your head. How about resting for a few minutes? Katie, can you and Melanie take Christina over to sit down for a while?"

Christina was startled. When riders fell off, they should get right back on again, unless they were really hurt. Everyone knew that. "But I have to get back on," Christina said.

"Not right now you don't," Mona said firmly. "I'm getting on her first."

Christina stood up straighter. She still felt a little shaky, but she knew she wasn't injured. "I'm fine, Mona," Christina protested. "I should get on her."

"Christina, the mare needs schooling. You are clearly unwilling to educate her with the crop, so I'm going to do it for you, and for her, before she gets completely out of hand," Mona said.

"Please don't hit her," Christina said. "You can make her do it without the crop, I know you can."

"I know how you feel about Sterling, but she needs discipline. You have to understand that letting her get away with running out at the fences is simply unacceptable. If we don't correct her when she misbehaves, Sterling will never know what is expected of her, and you will never be able to trust her. And she will never trust you." Mona looked hard at Christina. "I know what I'm talking about. Go over there and sit down for a minute. After I school her a little I'll put you back on her and you'll see the difference."

Katie and Melanie each took one of Christina's arms. Reluctantly she let them help her to the middle of the arena, where she sat down on a small wall jump. With a mixture of relief and anger, Christina watched as Mona put on her helmet, picked up the crop, and mounted Sterling.

"DON'T WORRY, CHRISTINA," KATIE SAID SYMPATHETICally. "Mona will get her to behave."

Christina couldn't answer. Her throat felt thick with angry tears. Mona was her instructor, and for a grown-up, she was a really special friend. Mona had gotten on Christina's pony many times to school him. So why should her getting on Sterling be any different?

"Hey, Chris, you still don't look so good. Why don't you take your helmet off for a minute?" Melanie suggested.

Christina realized she did feel hot and a little dizzy from her fall. She reached up and with trembling fingers managed to unsnap the chin strap of her safety helmet. It felt very heavy when she tried to lift it off her head, and she was grateful when Katie reached over and took it off for her.

Now her head felt cooler, but inside Christina was still upset. She concentrated on watching Mona trot Sterling around the ring at a very lively pace. At first Sterling appeared just as tense with Mona as she had been when Christina was riding her. But gradually the mare seemed to relax. After a few times around the ring, she lowered her head and let out a snort. Her trot rhythm became quieter as she stretched her neck out and began moving with smooth, even strides. Mona slid a hand forward and stroked the mare's neck, encouraging her to stay relaxed. She didn't seem to be using much pressure on the reins at all. Christina felt even angrier. Why couldn't Sterling be that good with her?

"Mona's such a great rider," Katie said with admiration.

"She sure is," Dylan agreed. He was sitting on the end of the wall jump next to Melanie.

Christina felt hurt. Did that mean that everyone thought Sterling was misbehaving because of the way Christina rode her?

Mona made Sterling walk and then accelerate into a canter. She cantered around the ring once, then headed for the first jump in the outside line. Christina hadn't seen anyone ride Sterling since the mare's last race in the spring. For just a moment she forgot her anger as she simply sat, entranced by her horse's graceful gaits. Sterling seemed to float above the ground instead of stepping on it, and Christina had the sensation that she was floating along with her. She felt herself rocking slightly in time with Sterling's canter as Mona approached the green vertical.

"Come on, come on, come on," Christina murmured in time with Sterling's canter as Mona rode up to the jump.

At the takeoff spot Christina held her breath. Would Sterling refuse the fence or run out, the way she had done with Christina? She cringed, expecting the worst. She hoped Mona wouldn't have to hit Sterling with the crop. But the mare cleared the vertical, her knees tucked neatly up toward her chin as she jumped the fence in perfect form. Christina watched Mona canter quietly down the line, putting in six even strides before clearing the next jump. It didn't look as though Mona had done anything at all, yet Sterling had behaved perfectly.

"She's being really good with Mona," Melanie observed innocently. "I wonder what the problem was before."

Christina shot her cousin a dirty look, but for once Melanie didn't seem to be taunting her. Melanie was toying with the tiny beaded braid in her pale blond hair, and her brown eyes were on the horse. Melanie was from New York, but her dad had sent her to stay with Christina's family for a while, mostly to keep her from getting into trouble. After a rocky start, Christina and Melanie were finally becoming friends.

"Sterling was probably just feeling fresh," Katie

said sympathetically. "You know how Thoroughbreds are. Even Seabreeze acts up sometimes." Seabreeze was Katie's seven-year-old bay mare.

Christina knew Katie was just trying to be nice. "Seabreeze never acts like that," Christina said quietly. "She's perfect."

"She bucked once," Katie tried. "At least I think it was a buck."

Christina rolled her eyes.

"Dakota used to run out like that with me when I first got him," Dylan said. Dakota was Dylan's Appendix quarter horse: half quarter horse, half Thoroughbred. He was a big-boned chestnut with four white socks and a white blaze.

Christina looked appreciatively at Dylan. "Really?" she asked, grateful for a chance to ignore Melanie and Katie. "What did you do?"

Dylan shoved his thumbs under the belt of his sand-colored chaps. "Well, at first I fell off him a lot," Dylan said with an embarrassed grin.

Christina was staring enchantedly at Dylan as she listened to him. She was remembering that during the school year he'd kept his straight brown hair longer, almost shoulder length, but this summer he'd cut it really short. Christina thought it made him look much older and handsomer.

"Of course I was only, like, nine years old or something," Dylan added.

Christina nodded, listening carefully.

"And my instructor had to get on him and school him for me a lot," Dylan went on. "Eventually he got better."

"Well, I'm sure your instructor helped, but obviously he got better because you're such a natural rider."

Christina tore her attention away from Dylan to see who had spoken. It was Cassidy. She had come over and was standing right next to Dylan. She was wearing a pair of expensive breeches and custom-made field boots that showed off her tall, slender build. Christina noticed she was also wearing makeup. It made her look much older than she probably was. Cassidy carelessly tossed back her perfectly cut blond hair and flashed a warm smile at Dylan, her green eyes glued on him. Dylan responded by smiling warmly back at Cassidy.

Christina put up a hand to smooth her own hair, which at the moment was gathered into a messy ponytail where it wasn't stuck to her sweaty head. Watching Cassidy talk easily with Dylan, she suddenly felt very, very small.

"Look, she's going to jump the liverpool," Melanie said.

Christina looked and saw Mona cantering toward the long rectangle of water flanked by two jump standards. This time Christina wasn't rooting for Sterling. Instead she found herself hoping that Sterling would misbehave, so that Dylan and the other kids would see that it wasn't Christina's riding that was causing the problem. For a second it looked as if Sterling might refuse to jump the water, but then she rocked back on her haunches and cleared it easily, giving her tail a swish as she landed as if she were glad to have it behind her.

"Bravo," Cassidy said. "I thought she was going to stop again."

"Why do horses hate water jumps so much?" Katie asked.

"I don't know," Dylan said. "It's funny, isn't it? They drink it every day, and most of them will walk right into a pond out in a pasture, but they don't want to jump over it or put their feet in a puddle."

"Well, it's a question of schooling, mostly," Cassidy said. "You just have to get them used to it. But of course there are some horses who hate water no matter what. You can make them jump it, as long as they don't have any bad experiences with it, but you always have to push them to get them to go over. And once they have a bad experience with a water jump, forget it," Cassidy said ominously. "My old instructor had this field hunter who hated water. Once he tried to quit before a liverpool, so my trainer gave him a smack. That made the horse lunge at the jump, and he caught the rail with his front legs," Cassidy said, demonstrating with her arms.

"What happened?" Katie asked.

"What do you think? He crashed through the

fence and landed in the water. It freaked him out, and after that you couldn't get him near a mud puddle! He'd just go crazy—rearing, bucking. But other than that, he was a nice horse," Cassidy added.

Christina didn't say anything. She hadn't known that a lot of horses were afraid to jump water. Then she remembered that when Sterling had been a racehorse, she'd hated to run in the rain or on a muddy track. Christina just hoped she and Sterling could make it through the water jump at the event.

She watched anxiously as Mona circled around and took the liverpool again. The horse pricked her ears forward and stretched, clearing the wide jump neatly. Christina wondered uneasily if Sterling would jump it the same way when she got back on the mare. Then Mona turned and rode a diagonal line up to the green rolltop jump, which was rounded just like a rolltop desk and set with a rail over it at three feet. Sterling jumped it willingly.

"She looks great, doesn't she?" Dylan observed.

Christina glanced quickly at Dylan. Was he talking about Mona or Sterling? But his eyes were on the horse, and she couldn't tell.

"That's a pretty nice horse," Cassidy said to Christina. "How long have you had her?"

"Not very long," Christina said.

"Is she off the track?" Cassidy asked.

Christina nodded. "My parents had some horses running up at Belmont, in New York. I found Sterling there."

"I thought so," Cassidy said.

*What did she mean by that?* Christina wondered. Did Sterling look like a racehorse instead of an Event horse?

"Christina saved her," Katie chimed in. "Sterling's groom was this really bad guy who used to hit her with a big wooden stick all the time."

"Oh, that's terrible," Cassidy said.

"Isn't it? Christina saw the guy doing it, but at first nobody believed her. Eventually they caught him doing it, and the owner fired him."

"Sterling's still really sensitive," Christina added. "She doesn't like strangers at all. Especially men."

"She's pretty," Cassidy said, watching Mona canter toward the outside line again from the opposite direction. "She's a nice mover. Of course, she could be a little better with her knees," Cassidy observed critically as Sterling jumped the fence.

"What do you mean?" Christina asked defensively. "Mona says she jumps great."

"Well, look at her motion," Cassidy pointed out. "She gets her knees up all right, but she doesn't really tuck her feet up underneath as much as she should."

"You're right," Dylan said, studying Sterling's form as she jumped the green vertical. "Hey, where'd you learn to ride?"

"I'm from Florida," Cassidy told them. "Miami. I learned to ride down there."

"You just moved up here, didn't you?" Katie asked. "I heard the grooms talking about your horses."

"Horses? How many do you have?" Melanie demanded.

"Two," Cassidy replied. "A hunter and a jumper, both geldings." She sighed. "I sure miss riding them."

Christina noticed Cassidy looking longingly at Sterling, and for a moment she felt sympathetic. She tried to imagine moving hundreds of miles away to a new state and having to leave her horse. "When are your horses coming?" she asked.

"They're being shipped up in a few weeks," Cassidy told them. "I hope they make the trip okay. I mean, I'm not worried about my jumper; he'll be fine. But my hunter's really green, and he's only four years old. He's never been on a long trailer trip."

"What's 'green'?" Melanie asked.

Cassidy raised one eyebrow for a moment, as if she was surprised at the question. "He's young. It just means he's still learning. But he's been going really nicely. My jumper's older," she added. "He's been around."

"What do you mean?" Melanie asked.

"You know, all the A-circuit shows," Cassidy said casually. "We did the Hampton Classic up in New York. And we did the National last October."

"Really?" Dylan said. He was looking at Cassidy with unmasked admiration.

"You mean you rode in the National Horse Show at Madison Square Garden in New York?" Melanie asked skeptically.

"Yeah," Cassidy said. "Last October."

"You rode at the Garden?" Katie exclaimed. "That is *so* cool!"

Christina and Melanie exchanged looks. For once she and her cousin were thinking the same thing. Was Cassidy telling the truth, or was she just trying to impress them? "How old are you?" Christina asked.

"Thirteen," Cassidy answered. "My birthday was last month."

Christina forgot all about watching Mona school Sterling. The National Horse Show at Madison Square Garden was one of the biggest, most famous horse shows in the United States. Christina dreamed of riding there one day. Cassidy would have to be a really good rider to qualify for the National. And she was only thirteen! Again Christina wondered if Cassidy was telling the truth.

"What'd you go in?" Dylan asked.

"I did the junior jumpers with Rebound," Cassidy said. "That's my jumper."

"How'd you do?" Christina asked.

"We won," Cassidy answered.

Christina thought back to the previous October, when she had been happily doing the pony hunter and jumper divisions at local shows and feeling very proud of herself. Cassidy was only a little older than she was, and she had been doing the big A-rated shows in the junior jumpers. The pony jumpers were nothing compared to that.

"What do you all show in?" Cassidy wanted to know. She addressed her question to all of them, but Christina noticed she was really looking at Dylan.

"I do equitation mostly," Katie told her. "And Seabreeze, my mare, has been doing well in some of the hunter divisions."

"And what about you, Dylan?" Cassidy asked.

"I do the children's eq, too," Dylan said. "But this spring and summer I've been training Dakota to do eventing."

"Oh, really? Eventing's so exciting," Cassidy said. "I have such respect for event riders. Have you started competing yet? I mean, I know you can't do most two- and three-day events until you're fourteen, but have you done any horse trials?"

Dylan nodded. "We did our first one this spring, at Foxwood Acres, just down the road." Dylan gestured in the direction of the neighboring farm. "It was so much fun! Especially the cross-country course. I think Dakota really got into it. We ended up getting fourth."

"That's so great," Cassidy gushed. "At your first event? Your horse must be so talented."

Christina remembered the event Dylan was

talking about. She had planned to ride in it, too, with one of Mona's horses, an Irish Thoroughbred named Foster. Christina had ridden Foster for weeks preparing for that event. Then she couldn't go, because her parents had made her go to New York with them. At the time she'd been bitterly disappointed at missing the event after all her hard work. But that wasn't the only thing: Dylan had asked her to the spring formal at Henry Clay Middle School, and she'd had to miss the dance, too. She still felt terrible whenever she remembered that, although Christina knew if she hadn't gone to New York, she'd never have found Sterling. And Sterling was the perfect horse, the beautiful gray mare she'd always dreamed of owning.

Or was she? Christina suddenly remembered that Mona was still on Sterling. She looked around for her helmet and saw that Katie was still holding it. She reached for it and pushed it on her head again, tucking in the sticky wisps of hair that had come loose from her ponytail.

"Christina, what do you show in?" Cassidy was asking her.

"Oh, I'm training Sterling to be an Event horse, too," Christina answered. "There's another event coming up in a couple of weeks. And I'm not going to miss this one," she added, glancing pointedly at Dylan.

"Oh, Dylan, are you riding in that event?" Cassidy asked.

Dylan nodded. "Hey, maybe you could come," he suggested to Cassidy.

"I'd love to," Cassidy said. "I just wish I had Rebound here. He'd love to do a little cross-country course like that. Do they have team competition at this event? It'd be great to be on your team, Dylan." She smiled at him, showing her perfectly straight teeth.

"We already have a team," Christina said quickly, before Dylan could answer. "Me and Katie and Dylan." She smiled at them. "Right, guys?"

"Right," Katie said.

"Oh," Cassidy said, sounding disappointed.

Christina stood up. It was time to get back on her horse.

"Listen, my horses aren't going to be shipped up here for another couple of weeks at least," Cassidy said as Christina headed toward Sterling. "So for the time being, I'm sort of stuck without anything to ride. Of course, Mona's been letting me ride Foster—"

"Foster?" Christina bristled. She hadn't known that Cassidy had been riding Foster. Of course, Christina didn't ride him anymore, now that she had Sterling to work with. But she had begged for a year to ride Foster, and only this spring had Mona finally let her get on him. Foster was Mona's best horse, and yet she had already let Cassidy, a complete stranger, ride him? Christina could hardly believe it. How could Mona do that?

"Yeah," Cassidy said. "I mean, he's nice and all, but he's really not my type. I like a more forward-going horse. Anyway, what I wanted to say was, I'd be glad to ride Sterling for you any time," Cassidy offered. "You know, if you're busy or whatever and you want somebody to school her. I can see she's got some problems right now, but I imagine she has great potential."

Christina could feel her ears turning hot with anger. First Mona had let this girl she hardly knew ride Foster; now the girl was criticizing Christina's beloved horse and acting as if just anyone could ride her. Christina could barely believe it. *And just what did she mean about Sterling having problems?*

Cassidy went on. "I really enjoy a challenge, so just let me know if you want me to get on her." Cassidy watched Sterling walking around with Mona. "She really could be a nice little horse," Cassidy mused. "It's too bad she's a quitter."

*Quitter?* The word stung Christina worse than the yellow jacket she'd accidentally put her hand on the other day. She jerked her head around and glared at Cassidy. How dare she call Sterling a quitter? She hadn't even seen the horse until just now. How could she act as though she knew so much about her?

But before she could answer, Dylan spoke. "You know, you could ride Dakota sometime, if you want," he suggested.

"Really? Oh, that would be great," Cassidy said. "Thank you!"

Christina stared at Dylan, astounded. They didn't know anything about Cassidy. They'd never even seen her ride. She was probably just bragging about all her horse show experience. How could Dylan offer to let her ride Dakota like that?

Dylan shoved his thumbs into the waistband of his chaps. "No problem," he said, smiling at Cassidy. "I mean, I'll just double-check with my parents, but they're not going to care. In fact, I've got a baseball tournament on Thursday, and I'll be gone the whole day. Can you ride Dakota for me then?"

"On Thursday? Sure," Cassidy said. "Why don't you show me where his tack is?"

Dylan and Cassidy got up and started toward the barn. Before they walked away, Cassidy turned around and said, "Oh—nice meeting you. I guess I'll be seeing you around, huh?"

Christina watched with dismay as they headed up the path together. Why was Dylan paying so much attention to Cassidy? Anyone could see she was just trying to impress them. And she had called Sterling a quitter right in front of everybody! Christina felt herself steaming with anger and indignation.

"Well, she seems nice, huh?" Katie said cheerfully.

"Nice?" Christina stared at Katie in disbelief. "What's so nice about her?"

Katie looked puzzled. "Well, I thought she was nice. Why, did I miss something?"

"Katie! Didn't you hear her? She called Sterling a quitter!"

Katie frowned. "I don't think she meant it like that."

"Yes, she did," Christina insisted. "She's mean—and a big snob, if you ask me. And she's probably making up that stuff about winning at the Garden! She's only talking to us because she likes Dylan. Can't you tell?"

"So you're upset because she's talking to your boyfriend?" Melanie said to Christina.

"My what?" Christina asked, astonished. She liked Dylan a lot, but he wasn't her boyfriend. "Dylan's my friend," she said carefully. "We're all friends. It's just that she has no business going off with him like that," Christina declared.

"What do you mean?" Katie asked.

"It's like she's trying to get him away from us or something. So she can have him all to herself," Christina said. "I think it's weird."

"Well, why don't you do something about it?" Melanie said.

"I don't think she was trying to get him away from us," Katie said uncertainly. "Dylan asked her to ride Dakota for him on Thursday, and he went to show her where Dakota's tack is. What's wrong with that?"

"If he was my boyfriend, I'd go with them," Melanie observed.

"He's not my boyfriend!" Christina snapped.

"Then why are you getting so upset?" Melanie asked coolly.

Christina opened her mouth to make some kind of retort, but no words would come out, so she closed it again. It seemed like everybody was against her today, even her horse.

"Christina," Mona called to her from across the ring. Mona had dismounted and was leading Sterling toward her.

Christina looked at Sterling, and for the first time ever, the thought of getting on a horse filled her with dread. How was she supposed to get ready for the event when she was nervous about getting on her own horse? And there was something else bothering her. Cassidy's remark about horses and water jumps stuck in her head. Sterling hated water. Christina knew she needed to school her over it, to prepare her for the water obstacle at the event, but what if she made a mistake? What if Sterling started freaking out about jumping water?

"Let's go, Chris. I want you to get on her while she's still got her schooling in her head," Mona said, interrupting Christina's doubt-filled thoughts. With a little sigh, Christina willed the butterflies in her stomach to be still and stepped grimly toward Sterling. Then with trembling fingers she took up the reins and let Mona give her a leg up.

THE FAMILIAR FEEL OF THE SADDLE UNDER HER WAS REASSURING, but Christina was still nervous. She adjusted her stirrups, noticing that she needed to shorten them only one hole from Mona's length.

Mona had noticed it, too. "You're getting so tall, Chris," she remarked.

Christina finished tucking the ends of the stirrup leathers into the keepers and shortened her reins. Then she looked at Mona and waited for instructions.

"When I first got on her she was pretty tense," Mona said, stroking Sterling's neck as she spoke. "I'm sure she was just reacting to your being a little nervous. Remember that even if you feel less than confident inside, you don't want to let your horse feel it in your body. So take deep breaths and keep telling yourself to relax," Mona told her. "That's half the battle right there."

"Did she try to run out when you were jumping her?" Christina asked anxiously.

Mona shook her head. "I was hoping she would misbehave with me so that I could get after her for it, but as soon as she relaxed, she was fine." Mona smiled at Christina. "Of course, you know how smart horses are. They always know that when an instructor gets on, they'd better behave."

"So what do I do if she acts up with me?" Christina asked.

"Just ride her like you're an instructor, and don't worry about it," Mona joked. Then she frowned. "Seriously, Christina, Sterling's a good horse. She wants to please you, but she has to know clearly and without any doubt what you expect from her. And you have to be prepared to show her that."

Christina was staring at a silver streak in Sterling's dark mane just in front of her withers. She knew what Mona was going to say next.

Mona held out the crop. "Here," she said. "I don't think you'll need this, but if you do need it and you're not carrying it, it's too late."

Christina stared at the crop. Then, reluctantly, she reached over and took it into her hand. In her head she knew Mona was right. A professional rider would always carry a "stick"—a crop or a whip of some kind. But it was all she could do to hold it in her hand. She couldn't imagine actually using it on Sterling. Sterling would think she was just as bad as the groom who had abused her in her racing days. Christina closed her fingers gingerly around the handle of the crop. She would carry it, because Mona said to, but she knew she wouldn't use it.

"You ready?" Mona asked.

Christina nodded.

"All right," Mona said with an encouraging smile. "Let's see you jump that outside line just like you would on your old pony." She gave Christina's thigh an affectionate pat. "Go ahead."

Christina looked toward the green vertical and nudged Sterling's sides with her legs. "Come on, Sterling," she whispered. "Just be a good girl—please?"

As if in answer, Sterling snorted and tossed her head a little from side to side as Christina pushed her right leg into Sterling's side and urged the mare into a canter. As she came around the turn toward the green vertical, Christina felt the butterflies stirring again but tried to ignore them.

"Relax, relax, relax," she whispered in time with Sterling's canter. She saw Sterling's ears flick forward and back, her attention shifting between Christina and the fence.

"That's it, Chris," she heard Mona say. "Now just keep your leg firmly closed and let the fence come to you."

*Let the fence come to you.* The words echoed in Christina's head, mixed in with Sterling's hoofbeats and the pounding of her own heart. Mona made it sound so easy. Christina looked over the vertical, pressing her legs into Sterling's sides. Then the fence was in front of her. Would Sterling jump it? For a moment all the sounds stopped. Christina suddenly realized that was because she and Sterling were in the air, sailing over the fence.

She felt the downward thrust of the landing as Sterling's front legs touched the ground again, and then her hind legs. Then the familiar sound of hoofbeats resumed as the horse cantered on toward the second jump.

*One, two, three, four, five, six.* Christina counted the strides in her head between the fences, and after the sixth came the quiet soaring sensation again as Sterling jumped the second fence.

"You're doing great, Christina," Mona encouraged. "Keep riding her just like that and you'll both be fine."

Christina's stomach was settling down again. She realized she'd been holding her breath, and she let it out and breathed in deeply. Sterling was cantering along quietly and calmly, waiting for Christina's next command.

"That was beautiful," Mona commented. "Do it again."

Christina circled the ring and jumped down the

outside line again. Sterling was quiet and willing, and Christina felt her confidence returning with each jump.

"Now take the rolltop." Mona indicated the fence toward the middle of the ring.

Christina looked for the fence, automatically using her right leg and left rein to cue Sterling to turn. She rode a diagonal line up to the rolltop and found herself smiling again as Sterling cleared it easily. She reached forward with one hand and rewarded the mare with a pat. "Good girl," she told the horse. "Good girl."

Sterling bobbed her head graciously under Christina's hand, as if she were acknowledging the compliment.

"You look great, Christina!" Katie called to her from the wall jump where she still sat with Melanie.

Christina smiled her thanks to her best friend and looked toward Mona for further instructions. She was relieved and delighted that Mona's schooling seemed to have corrected Sterling's behavior. Christina felt a little silly for having been angry at Mona. She should have trusted her.

"Now come around and take the liverpool," Mona instructed.

Christina nodded and looked down toward the other end of the ring. She was cantering on the right lead, headed for the water jump. As she came down the long side of the ring she saw Dylan and Cassidy strolling down the hill together toward the arena. For a second she was distracted. Were they holding hands?

"Look, look," Mona urged her. "Christina! Where are your eyes?"

Christina knew that Mona meant for her to look toward the jump. She tore her attention away from Dylan and Cassidy as she turned toward the liverpool. A little breeze rippled its surface, and she felt Sterling's whole body come to attention as she asked the mare to face the water jump.

"Right leg, right leg," Mona called.

Too late, Christina realized that she had misjudged the approach to the liverpool. She had cut the turn and ended up at an angle to the jump, when she should have come straight at it. It was wide already; if Sterling jumped it from that angle, she probably wouldn't clear it—she'd land with her feet in the water instead. And Sterling didn't like to put her feet in water.

Christina realized she might have just enough time to correct her approach and put Sterling straight at the jump. But before Christina could react, Sterling ducked her left shoulder and plunged to the right in an awkward sideways motion. Christina was nearly pitched over the mare's left shoulder, but she shoved her heels down and held on with her legs until she got herself centered in the saddle again.

"Halt." Mona's voice was low, but it carried.

Christina knew that tone. It meant that the rider

had made a foolish mistake. She pulled up and waited for Mona to say something.

"What happened there?" Mona asked quietly.

Christina felt frozen. She didn't know what to say or do. She finally just shrugged and stared at Mona's paddock boots. She could feel Mona's serious gray eyes on her, but she didn't meet her gaze.

"What happened?" Mona repeated.

Christina knew she was supposed to analyze her own mistake. "It was my fault," she muttered. "I didn't ride straight to the liverpool." She glanced back toward the fence rail and saw Dylan and Cassidy standing together watching. Quickly she looked back down at Sterling's withers.

"It looked like you just completely forgot what you were doing there for a second," Mona said. "Let's try to concentrate on the job, all right? Pick up a canter and come at it again, and this time keep your eyes in the direction you're going."

Without a word, Christina shortened her reins and picked up a trot. As she trotted past Katie and Melanie, she heard Melanie say, ". . . should have been looking at the fence," and she saw Katie nodding in agreement. It made her angry. She was sure neither one of them could do any better if they had to ride Sterling. Katie's mare, Seabreeze, was always perfect, and Melanie's horse, Pirate Treasure, an ex-racehorse gelding, was almost completely blind, so he never went very fast.

Then, as she picked up a canter and came down the long side of the ring, she had to pass Dylan and Cassidy. She couldn't help looking at them again, and though she didn't see them holding hands, she thought they were standing very close together—too close—and that bothered her.

Suddenly she didn't want to be there at all. She wished she could just stop and get off, but she knew she couldn't put Sterling away until she got her to jump the liverpool. "Come on, Sterling," she whispered through clenched teeth. "Let's get this over with."

As she turned off the rail toward the jump, she felt Sterling raise her head and slow down a little. Christina pressed her legs firmly into her horse's sides. She had been careful not to cut the turn on the approach, so they were coming straight at the water, just as they should be.

But Sterling's ears were pricked forward too much, a sign that she was nervous instead of just paying attention. Christina felt the mare's canter get slower and slower and knew if she didn't do something, Sterling would refuse or run out again. She nudged Sterling again with her legs, urging her to move on, but got no response.

"Stick! Stick!" Mona was saying. She meant for Christina to reinforce the message she was sending with her legs by giving Sterling a swat with her crop.

Christina knew Mona was right. Sterling had

already refused the liverpool once without getting reprimanded, so she would probably try to do it again. A horse should always respect the rider's leg commands, but Sterling was ignoring Christina's completely.

"Stick, Christina! Tap her with your crop!" Mona said.

"Come on, Sterling," Christina said desperately. She knew she should listen to Mona's advice and use the crop. But her arm felt frozen. She couldn't seem to make herself put the reins into the other hand so that she could reach back with her crop and use it on Sterling's rump. She did manage to give the horse a firm kick with her right leg, but it was too late. Sterling skidded to a momentary stop, then plunged to the right again to avoid jumping the liverpool.

". . . too much horse for her to handle . . ." Cassidy's voice carried across the ring, and Christina heard, although she knew she wasn't meant to.

Christina pulled up again. She felt all the blood drain from her face at the same time that her heart began to pound. Her hands trembled as she gathered up the reins and prepared to come at the jump again. She knew if she thought about it too much, she'd discover that she was terrified, so she pushed the thought out of her head and focused on her anger instead. Sterling was the beautiful gray mare she'd always dreamed of owning. Why was she doing this to Christina? Everyone would think that what Cassidy said was true: Her horse was a quitter.

Then Mona was beside her. She put a hand on Sterling's reins to hold her steady and said to Christina, "Let me get on her."

Christina looked into Mona's eyes. Except for the tiniest crinkle of a frown between her eyebrows, Mona's expression was unreadable, which meant she wasn't pleased with Christina. But Mona would never say that. Christina had learned from years of working with her that Mona would never yell. If Christina behaved inappropriately, Mona would simply excuse her from the lesson, or the showring, until she was ready to act right.

"Christina, dismount, and let me get on her," Mona repeated.

Christina knew Mona expected her to obey. More important, she knew she should respect Mona's experience with horses and follow her instructions always. She should have tapped Sterling with the crop before, and she hadn't. Now Mona was asking her to dismount and let her get on Sterling for the second time in half an hour.

Christina had never disobeyed Mona. She had never even doubted Mona, not for a second. In her head she knew she should simply dismount and let Mona school the horse. It would be better for her, and better for Sterling. But all the kids were watching. Dylan was watching. And Cassidy was watching.

What would they all think of her? *They'll think you can't ride your own horse,* Christina told herself. Would they be right?

Christina couldn't look at Mona. *Quitter!* The word echoed in Christina's head, and she wasn't sure if Cassidy had said it again or if it was her own heart talking to her—because she realized she didn't want to stay on Sterling. And at the same time she knew she had to, or she'd be a quitter, too.

"Christina, give me the horse," Mona said firmly.

Christina slowly looked up. "No," she said. "I can do it."

"Chris, it's too late. You've already shown Sterling she can get away with running out. Now she's just going to be worse. Let me get on her," Mona said.

"No!" Christina said again. "I'm going to make her do it myself."

Mona was shaking her head. "Maybe you're just having a bad day, and that's okay. But right at this moment you are not in any shape to jump this horse. Please dismount," she said. "Now."

Christina hesitated for a second. Then she made up her mind. She was going to jump Sterling over the liverpool. She thumped her horse's sides with her heels and moved into a canter. It was a little fast, but she thought that was okay—the faster she was moving, she figured, the easier it would be to get the mare to jump the water.

"What's she doing?" Katie said, sounding amazed.

What *was* she doing? Christina wondered. She was defying her instructor, for one. She was also going to prove to everyone, including herself, that she could ride her own horse.

"Christina Reese, bring your horse into the center of the ring, *now*," Mona said sharply.

But Christina's eyes were locked on the water jump. She kept her fingers clenched around the reins, to stop them from trembling, and she kept thumping Sterling's sides with her legs to keep her cantering strongly at the liverpool. She was afraid of losing her nerve, so she concentrated on staying angry. At least that made her feel strong. She tried to focus on how badly she wanted to ride in the event at Foxwood Acres. "I'm not letting one stupid water jump keep me from competing," she muttered.

"Christina, *halt*," Mona commanded.

Christina rode on. She was determined to make Sterling go over the water. Five strides before the liverpool she felt Sterling slow down, just as she had before. She dug her right leg firmly into the mare's side. *"Get up,"* she growled.

But Sterling had gotten away with running out and was going to try it again. Christina felt her trying to turn past the fence again. This time, though, she set her left hand and kept Sterling's head facing the jump as she kicked her again with her right leg to keep her hindquarters in line.

Surprised, Sterling tossed her head and tried to

turn away once more. But Christina was ready for it. She gave a firm tug on the left rein to keep Sterling from going to the right and avoiding the jump.

Sterling half reared, her front legs lifting off the ground in protest at having her mouth yanked. Christina felt a surge of fear. Would Sterling rear up and fall over on her? But a second later the mare planted her front legs and balked, looking for an escape from jumping.

"She's afraid to use her stick."

Again she recognized Cassidy's voice. And somehow she forgot that she had promised herself never to hit Sterling. Christina was as angry as she had ever been. How could her horse be doing this to her right in front of everyone? She'd show Cassidy that Sterling was no quitter. And neither was she. In the midst of Sterling's obstinate rearing and balking, Christina managed to get her reins into one hand and bring her stick down on her horse with her right hand.

She had meant to give her a medium tap. That should have been hard enough for a sensitive horse. But adrenaline powered her arm, and she ended up giving Sterling a firm smack.

Sterling exploded. She was half a stride from the takeoff spot, but she took off anyway, launching herself over the liverpool. Christina was left behind as the mare made a huge effort to jump the water. She tried to bend forward to catch up with the horse's motion and simultaneously tried to let the reins slip through her fingers so she wouldn't yank on Sterling's mouth, but her reactions were a second too late.

Sterling came down with one front foot in the water and stumbled, catching the rail with her hindquarters and bringing the whole thing down into the water with her. The splashing startled her, and she lunged forward, kicking the fallen rail with a hind leg and tripping on the lip of the twelve-inch-deep rectangle of water with a front leg. Christina felt her feet come out of the stirrups as her legs swung back, and she was pitched forward onto Sterling's neck as the mare fought frantically to clear herself of the rail and the water.

"Sit up, Christina!" Mona's voice was urgent. "Sit up and pull the reins!"

But Christina couldn't seem to get herself back into the saddle. For the second time that day she found herself lying on her mare's neck. But this time Sterling panicked. She was a racehorse, bred for speed, and she began to run.

"Omigosh!"

Christina heard Katie's alarmed voice. Oddly, she wasn't afraid herself. Sterling was flying around the ring as if she were coming down the homestretch at Belmont. Christina made one more effort to sit up and find the reins, but she was too far forward on the mare's neck. She simply couldn't get her legs down so that she could pick up her hands and stop Sterling.

"She's going to jump the fence!" Melanie said.

Christina heard that and realized that Sterling was heading for the outside line again, at a dead run. She was terrified—she knew she was going to fall off, *wished* she would hurry up and fall off. But she was completely helpless. As Sterling's mane whipped her face and hoofbeats pounded in her ears, all Christina could do was watch the ground rush by underneath her and wait for the fall. As scared as she was, it struck her as funny.

Then an instant later she felt Sterling heave herself into the air, and caught a glimpse of the green vertical underneath her as the horse jumped the fence. Christina was thrown over the horse's right side. It was a relief to finally be falling off. Christina had a curious, tumbling view of the mare's belly and hind legs cantering over her while she waited for the impact. She had just a split second to be mildly amazed that she hadn't been stepped on, then she felt all the air rush out of her lungs as she met the ground in a bone-jarring thud.

DUST.

There was no air, only dust. Christina wanted air, but it seemed that dust filled her eyes, her nose, her lungs. She sucked at it uselessly but couldn't catch her breath. Dimly, through the cloud of dust, she saw feet, Mona's feet, and someone else's.

She wanted to ask someone to please give her some air, but when she mouthed the words, no sound came. She clutched the ground with her fingers and tried to get up, but something hurt somewhere. If she could just breathe, she thought distractedly, she could figure out where.

"Lie still, Christina."

Mona's soothing voice was telling her to be still, and she tried, but somehow her limbs kept creeping into motion. She still couldn't breathe, and it was agony, and the dust was awful. And something hurt, something *hurt!*

As soon as she finally managed to fill her lungs with air she let it out in a groan of pain.

"It's okay, Chris, you're going to be okay," Mona was telling her as she knelt beside her. "You just got the wind knocked out of you."

"Is she okay?" That was Katie.

"Wow, did that look like a hard landing." That was Melanie.

"Christina? Are you okay?" That was Dylan.

Christina tried to focus on her friends' faces but couldn't. It almost seemed as if all the voices were just coming out of the sky. She had the sensation that she was floating, and the sharp pain she'd felt somewhere a minute ago had gone away.

"Guys, back off and give her some room," Mona said. "Christina? Talk to me, please."

Mona's face with her short brown hair under her baseball cap appeared over Christina. Christina made an effort to clear her vision and say something, but it was too hard.

"Chris? How do you feel?" Mona asked.

Christina blinked. Suddenly she wasn't floating anymore; she could feel the hard ground underneath her now. She looked around and saw Katie and Dylan peering anxiously at her, while Melanie stood a little way back, looking worried.

"I'm fine," Christina said, struggling to sit up.

But when she tried to push herself to a sitting position, the pain came back, sharp and sure, and it was in her left wrist. "Ow!" she yelped, grabbing her left forearm and hugging it to her.

"What is it?" Mona asked.

"My wrist," Christina said. "It really hurts." It was a combination of sharp pain and tingling numbness that she had never felt before.

"Let me see," Mona said.

Gingerly Christina held out her left hand. There was a red lump on the outside of her wrist that seemed to be swelling before her eyes.

"I bet it's broken," Katie exclaimed.

"Katie, shush," Mona said. She carefully examined Christina's wrist. "Are you hurt anywhere else?" she asked.

"No," Christina said. "Just my wrist."

"Well, let's get you up, and then we'll see about getting it checked out," Mona said cheerfully. "I hope you just banged it when you fell, but we don't want to take any chances."

Christina held her arm close to her body and let Mona help her up. She found it humiliating that she actually needed help. She was used to bouncing right back up again when she fell off. This was the first time she'd ever really been hurt.

"Melanie," Mona said, "would you run up to the barn and see if you can reach Mike or Ashleigh?"

Melanie nodded and ran off up the hill. "Oh, no,"

Christina protested. "Do we have to call my parents?"

"Yes, we have to call your parents," Mona said firmly. "You need to go get your wrist X-rayed."

Christina had been to the emergency room once before, when she was about five. She had cut her head on a rock when she fell off her pony, and had gotten a few stitches over her eyebrow. The thought of going to the emergency room again didn't appeal to her at all. "I think it's going to be fine," Christina said. "Probably I just bumped it really hard, like you said. It feels better already," she lied.

"Christina, you're going to get it checked out, and that's final," Mona told her firmly.

Feeling squeamish, Christina let Mona and Katie help her up. Halfway up the hill to the barn she remembered her horse. "Who's taking care of Sterling?" she asked.

"I asked Cassidy to take her up to the barn and put her away," Mona said. "Don't worry about Sterling. I've got a spare stall, so she can stay here as long as she needs to."

"Thanks," Christina said. Sterling lived at Whitebrook Farm, her parents' Thoroughbred training and breeding farm just down the road. Christina had ridden Sterling over to Mona's for her lesson that morning, as usual. She had been worried about how she was going to get her back home. She was grateful to Mona for offering to let Sterling stay, but she didn't like the idea of Cassidy handling her horse. "Did you tell Cassidy how she is with strangers?" Christina asked anxiously.

"I feel sure that Cassidy can handle putting Sterling away," Mona said.

"She still tries to bite sometimes, if she's startled or if she doesn't know a person," Christina reminded her.

"Chris, she'll be fine," Mona insisted. "Now stop worrying about her."

"Okay," Christina said. But inside she was wondering how she was ever going to stop worrying.

A few hours later Christina was sitting gloomily in the passenger seat of her father's silver pickup truck, her left arm in a cast up to her elbow. The X ray had showed a small fracture in her wrist; she would have to wear the big cast for two weeks, then they'd take that one off and put a smaller brace on just her wrist. Mike Reese, her father, kept giving her sympathetic looks as they drove back to Whitebrook. But Christina was in no mood for sympathy.

"How does your wrist feel now, honey?" her dad asked, his blue eyes full of concern.

Christina sighed. "Dad, you just asked me that five minutes ago. It feels the same, okay?"

"I'm sorry," he said sincerely. "It's just that when you're a parent and your kid gets hurt, you always wish it were you instead. Besides, you look so miserable, it's pretty hard not to feel sorry for you."

"I am miserable," Christina said. "I can't believe I did such a stupid thing."

"What do you mean?" Mike asked. "You didn't plan to fall off. It's just one of those things you have to expect once in a while. Really, I'm amazed you haven't been hurt more, what with that nutso pony you were so fond of," Mike joked.

"Maybe I should stick to ponies," Christina said morosely. "I don't seem to be able to ride horses very well. And at least with ponies you're a lot closer to the ground if you fall off."

"Chrissy," her dad chided her gently. "You're a beautiful rider, you know that."

"Then how come I fell off twice in one day and I can't even get my own horse over a stupid jump?" Christina said angrily, her voice wavering with the tears she was trying not to let out.

"These things happen," Mike said. "Even experienced riders fall off. Think how many times your mom has fallen off racehorses."

That was true, Christina reflected. Her mom, Ashleigh Griffen, was one of the top jockeys in the country. And she had fallen off and been injured from time to time, though never too seriously.

Mike was shaking his head. "On second thought, don't remind me," he said. "It just about gives me heart failure every time she takes a spill."

Moments later they were turning up the gravel drive that led to Whitebrook Farm. Christina gazed at the familiar red barns and outbuildings set against the deep green backdrop of hilly pastures lush with Kentucky bluegrass. On one of the hillsides was a fallen spruce tree that she had jumped Sterling over many times. *How long will it be before I can jump it again?* she wondered sadly.

She was still asking herself the same question hours later at the dinner table, staring at her plate. The phone rang, and Ashleigh got up to answer it. Christina could hear her mother talking in the living room.

"Yes, about four weeks, maybe five, depending. She'll get a smaller brace in two weeks. The doctor said he'll know more then, when they X-ray it again," Ashleigh was saying.

Christina wondered who was asking about her. She cocked her head, trying to hear better.

"No, I didn't hear her say," Ashleigh went on. "But she's sitting right here. Just a minute." Ashleigh brought the cordless phone into the kitchen and handed it to Christina. "Mona," she said, nodding at the phone.

"Hello?" Christina said.

"Hi, Chris," Mona said. "Your mom tells me you're going to be in a cast for a few weeks."

"Yeah," Christina said glumly.

"How does it feel?"

"The cast is bugging me a lot more than my wrist," Christina said. "It's all the way up to my elbow. The doctor says it's not a bad break, but because of where it is I have to be extra careful not to injure it worse."

"That's too bad," Mona said sympathetically. "Oh, well, the time will go by before you know it," she said in a cheerful voice.

"I guess," Christina said. Adults always said things like that. Four or five weeks was practically one third of a whole summer. It seemed like an eternity.

"Listen, Christina, I was just telling your mom that Sterling's fine over here for now. She can stay as long as she needs to, and I'll be sure she gets turned out a lot."

"Thanks," Christina said.

"But she'll still need to be ridden pretty much every day. Have you thought about who you might get to exercise her for you?"

In fact, Christina hadn't thought about it at all. But Mona was right. Even if Sterling got turned out in a paddock every day, she'd still need to be ridden frequently, or she'd really backslide in her training. Christina thought how hard she'd been working with Sterling, training for the event. And now she couldn't ride for at least four weeks. The thought filled her with dismay.

"Chris? Are you there?" Mona asked.

"Yeah," Christina said.

"Well?"

"I—I hadn't really thought about it until now," Christina admitted. "Can't you take care of exercising her for me?" Christina didn't like the thought of anyone else riding Sterling, but Mona was the best person to do it.

"I wish I could," Mona said. "But I'm already riding three horses for other people right now, plus my two three-year-olds, plus my gelding," Mona said. "And then there's Foster. Between riding those seven horses and my teaching schedule, I just don't have the time to take on Sterling, too."

"But who else can ride her?" Christina asked. She had been certain that Mona would take care of Sterling for her.

"Well, if you don't know of anyone offhand, I have a suggestion." Mona waited.

"Who?" Christina asked.

"Cassidy Smith. She's a very experienced rider, and right now she has the time, because her horses won't be arriving up here for another few weeks. I think she'd be the best rider for Sterling, under the circumstances. And she's willing to do it. I already spoke to her."

"No." Christina felt a surge of anger. Cassidy had just moved to town! They knew almost nothing about her. How could Mona be suggesting that a girl she hardly even knew be allowed to ride Sterling?

"Why not?" Mona asked.

Christina heard Mona's carefully neutral tone and realized that Mona was probably not going to be pleased with her. She groped for an answer. "Because—because I have someone else I want to ask first," Christina finally said. She didn't really, but she'd come up with someone. Anyone would be better than Cassidy!

"Oh. Well, I didn't realize you had someone else in mind already," Mona said. "Who is it?"

Christina hesitated. "I know a couple of people. I'll have to talk to them and see who can do it."

"All right, then," Mona said. "But you need to let me know as soon as possible. In the meantime, I'll put Sterling on a turnout schedule."

"Okay," Christina said. "I'll get back to you soon."

"You do that," Mona said. "And Chris?"

"Yes?"

"If your other friends can't do it, please keep Cassidy in mind. She's a lovely, capable rider. She'll be good for Sterling," Mona said.

*She's a stuck-up, bragging boyfriend stealer and I wouldn't let her ride my horse if my life depended on it!* Christina thought angrily. "Yeah, well, I'm pretty sure I have someone else," she lied. "Thanks anyway."

"Okay, Christina." Mona sighed. "Feel better. I'll talk to you tomorrow."

"Okay, bye," Christina said.

She mashed the off button with her thumb and set

down the phone. Then she stared at her plate. She had hardly touched her dinner, but now she didn't feel like eating at all.

"What was that all about?" Melanie asked, munching an ear of fresh corn.

"Mona wanted to talk about who's going to exercise Sterling," Christina said. "Can you believe she wanted that Cassidy girl to do it?"

"No way," Melanie said.

"Who's Cassidy?" Mike asked. "I never heard you mention her before."

"She's this new girl," Melanie explained to her uncle.

"As if I would let somebody like her ride my horse," Christina said in disgust.

"What do you mean, 'somebody like her'?" Ashleigh asked. "What's the matter with her?"

"She just moved here, and she's already acting like she's the queen of Gardener Farm," Christina said.

"We met her today, and she was bragging all about how she rode at the Hampton Classic, and all these big shows," Melanie said.

"She said she won the junior jumpers at the Garden," Christina said. "Can you believe that?"

"Well, maybe she did," Ashleigh commented. "Do you have some reason to think she's lying?"

Christina and Melanie exchanged looks.

"You could always look it up, you know," Ashleigh went on. "All the standings from those big shows are recorded." She waited.

Christina didn't say anything.

Ashleigh went on, "If she did win the junior jumpers at the Garden, she'd have to be a very good rider."

Christina looked at her mother. Ashleigh's dark hair was pulled into a hasty ponytail that made her look young enough to be Christina's big sister instead of her mother. They had the same hazel eyes, except at that moment Ashleigh's eyes were questioning, and Christina's showed her discomfort. At last Christina had to look away.

"It's not really fair to assume bad things about someone you just met, is it?" Ashleigh asked gently. "Mona seems to think Cassidy is the best person to exercise Sterling for you. Someone's got to ride the horse. Mona knows you and Sterling very well—I can't imagine her choosing someone incompetent to ride your horse."

"She's not riding Sterling, and that's final!" Christina said. "I'll get someone to do it."

"Chrissy, why are you getting so worked up about this?" her father asked.

Christina glared at him. "Dad, please don't call me Chrissy! You know I hate it."

"Sorry," Mike said.

She stood up and picked up her plate. "May I be excused?" Christina demanded.

"Can I have your corn?" Melanie asked.

Christina picked up the ear of corn and plopped it

on her cousin's plate. Then she waited for her father to excuse her.

"You're excused," Mike said.

Christina took her plate to the sink and went outside, letting the screen door slam behind her. She was angry and upset, which seemed to make her wrist throb. She stomped down the path to the barns, not really caring where she ended up. Why did everyone think Cassidy was so great? And why did everyone seem to think that she was the only person who could ride Sterling?

Soon Christina found herself at one of the paddocks where the foals were turned out. She climbed up the fence, awkwardly protecting her injured wrist, and sat on the top rail. Maybe watching the babies play would make her feel better. Eleven little colts and fillies stopped their games to stare at Christina sitting on the fence. Then they wheeled, their fluffy baby tails twitching as they ran away, pretending to be terrified. They bolted to the far end of the paddock and then just as suddenly stopped and turned around to see what she was doing. Almost immediately they began to walk back toward her, overcome with curiosity. Christina couldn't help laughing.

She sat there for a while, watching the babies and thinking about Cassidy. She had to admit, Cassidy hadn't really acted stuck-up. She'd just looked so cool and acted so grown-up, with her dressy riding clothes and her makeup. Maybe Christina was being unfair, as Ashleigh had suggested. But then Christina remembered how Cassidy had hung on Dylan's every word and how Dylan had seemed so interested in her. She remembered hearing Cassidy say that Sterling was too much horse for her to handle, and she grew angry all over again.

She would never let Cassidy ride Sterling. "I can handle my own horse better than anybody!" Christina muttered fiercely. She watched the foals, who came tentatively closer and closer to her, their curiosity overwhelming their instinct to run away. Christina sat perfectly still while they approached. One of them, a little chestnut, bolder than the others, came right up to her and began nuzzling her foot.

"I'll find someone else to ride my horse," Christina said aloud. The foal started at her voice and bolted for the other end of the paddock. The rest of the young horses followed in a thunder of miniature hoofbeats, leaving Christina all alone. "But who?" she wondered.

"HEY, WHAT HAPPENED TO YOU?"

Christina jumped. She had been deep in thought and hadn't noticed anyone coming down the path. She turned and saw Kevin McLean's familiar tan, freckled face and auburn hair. "You scared me," she said indignantly.

"Sorry," Kevin said. He held a basketball under one arm and was all sweaty from playing. But there was concern in his green eyes and in his voice as he said again, "What happened to you?"

Christina sighed. "I sort of fell off Sterling," she said. Then she explained how she'd broken her wrist.

Kevin was a few months younger than Christina. The two had grown up together and were best friends, as close as brother and sister—closer, probably, Christina reflected, because they didn't live under the same roof. The McLeans lived in the smaller, older stone house just across from the Reeses' big white farmhouse. Kevin's father, Ian McLean, had been the head trainer at Whitebrook for nearly fourteen years.

"Wow. Bummer," Kevin said sympathetically when Christina had finished telling him what had happened. "Who's going to ride Sterling while your arm's in a cast?" he asked.

As usual, Kevin had gotten straight to the point. "I don't know yet," Christian said. "That's what I've been trying to figure out."

"Did you ask Katie?" Kevin suggested.

Christina shook her head. "I haven't asked anyone yet. I'm going to ask Katie, but I don't really think she'll be able to do it. She's got Seabreeze, and anyway, Sterling's not the kind of horse just anyone can ride."

Kevin nodded and twirled the basketball between his fingers. "I know what you mean."

"Would you do it?" Christina asked hopefully. Kevin was a good rider. He had an Anglo-Arabian gelding named Jasper that he rode around the farm. Kevin didn't like competing in horse shows, but he had ridden for as long as Christina and could handle just about any kind of horse. She would definitely trust Kevin to ride Sterling.

"I don't know, Chris," Kevin said. "You know I'm not really into the kind of riding you like to do. Anyway, I've got baseball," he added.

Kevin was a sports fanatic. He was on two different baseball teams, and when he didn't have a ball game, he was rock climbing, in-line skating, or playing basketball with his friends. Christina knew he hardly had time to keep Jasper exercised, never mind Sterling.

She sighed. "What am I going to do?"

"I could ride her for you a couple of times, I guess," Kevin offered. "But I can't really promise to do it every day." He twirled the ball absently, thinking. "Isn't there anyone else who can do it? What about Mona?"

Christina shook her head. "Mona's too busy—she already told me. She wants me to let this new girl do it."

"Cassidy Smith," Kevin said.

"How do you know her?" Christina said in surprise.

"She's been to a few of our ball games." Kevin shrugged. "I guess she's a friend of Dylan's or something." Kevin and Dylan were on one of the same baseball teams.

Christina felt as though she'd been punched in the stomach. She'd thought that Dylan had just met Cassidy that day. She hadn't realized they'd been hanging out together.

"She seems pretty nice," Kevin said. "Why can't Cassidy ride Sterling for you?"

"Because I don't want her to," Christina snapped. "Why does everyone think she's so great, anyway?"

Kevin stopped twirling the ball. He looked at Christina intently. "I didn't say she was so great. I said she seems nice. Why, is there something I don't know about her?"

Christina shrugged and looked back at the foals, who were chasing each other around the paddock, practicing bucks. "Has she been hanging out with Dylan a lot?" she asked guardedly.

"Some," Kevin said vaguely. "Hmmm, do I sense a hint of jealousy in the air?"

"Why should I be jealous?" Christina asked airily.

"Um, because everyone knows you and Dylan have a thing for each other, and now there's this new girl who's getting all the attention," Kevin said frankly.

"I don't have a *thing* for Dylan," Christina argued. "He's my friend, and I'm just *interested* in what's going on between him and Cassidy, that's all. What's wrong with that?"

"Nothing," Kevin said. "If he's your friend, why don't you ask him yourself about Cassidy?"

Christina scowled.

"Well, I have to get home," Kevin said. "Let me know what happens with Sterling. If I can help you out with her, I will."

"Thanks, Kev," Christina said.

He walked several steps away, then turned around. "Christina," he said.

"What?"

"Dylan's not really into Cassidy. She's pretty and nice and all, but he still likes you," Kevin told her.

Christina could feel herself start to blush from her ears to her toes. "Oh, I'm so sure," she said sarcastically. But inside she hoped it was true.

When Kevin had gone, Christina carefully climbed down from the fence and went back to the house. Just as she came in, the phone was ringing. "Christina, for you," her dad said, handing her the phone. "And Dylan called," he added.

Christina's heart did a little flip-flop. She took the phone and went upstairs to her room. "Hello?" she said.

"It's me," Katie said. "How's your arm?"

"Broken," Christina said. "Well, actually it's my wrist. But I have a cast all the way up to my elbow."

"Oh, no," Katie said. "Does it hurt much?"

"No, not much," Christina said. "It's just annoying. Listen, Katie, I was talking to Mona a while ago. I'm going to need someone to exercise Sterling for me until I can ride again. Would you be able to do it?" Christina asked.

"Me? Sterling? Oh, Christina, I don't think I can," Katie said. "I mean, she's not that simple to ride, and she's really used to you. Plus I've got Seabreeze to take care of. I'm really sorry," she added.

"That's okay," Christina said. "I figured you'd say that, but I thought I'd ask you anyway."

"Sorry," Katie said again.

Christina knew she really meant it. "It's okay. Katie?"

"Yeah?"

"Do you think Dylan would ride her for me if I asked him?" Christina asked.

There was a pause. Then Katie said, "He might. You should definitely ask him."

"I guess I will," she said. "My dad said Dylan called a while ago. I'm going to call him back right now before I chicken out."

"Okay. Call me back and tell me what he says," Katie said eagerly.

"I will. Bye," Christina said.

"Bye," Katie said.

Christina dialed Dylan's number. His mom answered. "Hi, Mrs. Becker, this is Christina Reese. May I speak with Dylan, please?"

"Oh, hello, Christina," Mrs. Becker said. "Just a minute—he's about to go out. A friend's mother is picking him up. But I think he's still waiting on the front porch."

Christina waited. She heard voices, then a door closing. Then Dylan's voice.

"Christina?"

"Hi," Christina said, feeling nervous and wishing she didn't. She used to talk to Dylan on the phone all the time, when they were first getting to know each other. But for some reason, ever since she hadn't been able to go to the spring formal with him, he hadn't called her as much, and she felt awkward calling him.

"What's up?" Dylan asked.

Christina hesitated. "My dad said you called me."

"Sure. I called to see how your wrist was. Your dad told me it was broken. That's too bad," Dylan said.

"Yeah," Christina agreed. There was silence. Desperately she tried to think of something else to say. "Um, so, where are you going?" she asked.

"To a movie," Dylan said.

"Oh. Which one?" Christina asked, wishing she were brave enough to suggest meeting Dylan there. But she didn't know whom he was going to the movie with, and she didn't want to ask him. She thought it would sound like she was being nosy.

"It's that new movie, the one with Sharon Flake and Bradley Ridley-Roberts," Dylan said.

"Oh, Bradley Ridley-Roberts is such a great actor," Christina said. "Don't you think?"

"Sure," Dylan said.

He sounded distracted, Christina thought. She decided to just jump in and ask him, before she lost her nerve. "Um, Dylan? I was wondering. . . ."

"Yeah?"

"I'm going to need someone to exercise Sterling for me for a few weeks until I can ride again." She took a deep breath and hurried on. "I was wondering if you'd be willing to do it." She squeezed her eyes shut as she waited for a reply.

"Me?"

*What did he mean by that?* Christina wondered in a panic. "Um, yeah," she said uncertainly. "I mean, I know you're busy with baseball and all, and you have Dakota, but Sterling's just coming along so well with her training—well, except for those runouts, but that was really my fault. She needs an experienced rider, but Mona's too busy, and Katie can't, and Kevin said he could do it once in a while, but—"

"I'd like to help you out with her," Dylan said, "but I just don't have the time right now. Maybe I could ride her now and then," he offered.

"Oh," Christina said, feeling her heart sink. "Well, okay. Thanks anyway."

"Listen, why don't you ask Cassidy Smith?" Dylan suggested.

*Great,* Christina thought. *Here we go again with Cassidy.* She wished she could have just one conversation the whole day in which somebody didn't bring up Cassidy Smith.

"She's a great rider," Dylan went on. "And she already offered to ride Sterling for you anyway."

Christina forced herself to say, "Yeah, maybe . . ."

"Mona said Cassidy could ride Foster in the event, but since you need somebody to work with Sterling—"

Cassidy riding Foster in the event? What was he talking about? "What do you mean?" Christina interrupted.

"Well, obviously you're not going to be able to

ride with our team, now that you've broken your wrist," Dylan said.

For the first time Christina thought about what that meant. If she couldn't compete in the event, Dylan and Katie couldn't, either—unless they found a third rider to take Christina's place.

"Cassidy said she would take your place, so that Katie and I can still compete in the horse trial," Dylan explained. "She was going to ride Foster, but I just thought maybe you'd want her to ride Sterling, since you need somebody to exercise her anyway."

Christina was shocked. She could see how Dylan would want to go on and ride in the event, but he and Katie and Christina were a team—how could he be talking about replacing her, just like that? She was still trying to come up with a response when she heard Mrs. Becker calling.

"Dylan? Cassidy's mom is here."

Cassidy's mom? Why would Cassidy's mom be picking up Dylan? Christina wondered. Then it sank in. Dylan was going to the movies with Cassidy. Christina was speechless.

"I have to go," Dylan said. "I'll see you around, right?"

"Right." Christina barely got the word out. Dylan was going to the movies with Cassidy. And he wanted Cassidy to ride in her place on the event team. She managed to say good-bye, then turned off the phone with her thumb and flopped backward onto her bed, letting the phone drop. "I wish I'd fallen on my head," Christina said miserably. "Then at least I wouldn't know about it."

"Know about what?"

Christina looked over and saw Melanie standing in the doorway of her room. "That Dylan's going out with Cassidy. I just found out," Christina said bitterly, staring at the ceiling. She hadn't meant to cry, but she felt a tear ooze out of the corner of each eye anyway and roll down her temples, splashing on her ears.

"Oh," Melanie said. "Wow. Sorry."

Melanie could be tough and hard to reach, but Christina thought she heard actual sympathy in her voice. "Thanks," Christina whispered.

"Did you get anyone to ride Sterling for you yet?" Melanie asked.

"No," Christina said, her voice beginning to choke with emotion. "And get this—now Cassidy's going to take my place on the team with Dylan and Katie."

As soon as she said it out loud, it hurt fifty times more, and she broke into real tears. "How could they do that?" Christina sobbed. "I can't even believe this whole thing happened. How could they just replace me like that? And what am I going to do about Sterling? How could she be so good for weeks and weeks, and then just suddenly turn into such a nightmare?"

Melanie laughed.

"What's so funny?" Christina said furiously, turning to look at her cousin.

"What you said," Melanie answered. "Sterling: night-mare? Get it?"

Christina had to think for a few moments, then she got the joke. She managed a small smile through her tears, but she didn't really feel any better. In fact, the more she thought about it, the worse she felt.

"First I practiced and practiced on Foster getting ready for the event in May, and then I didn't get to go," Christina sobbed.

"But at least you got Sterling. If you hadn't gone to New York, you never would have found her," Melanie pointed out.

"I know," Christina said. "But I've been training so hard to be ready for this event and now I won't be able to go again, because of this stupid cast," she exclaimed. She flung her arm backward against the bed and winced as the bump sent a wave of pain through her wrist.

"Take it easy," Melanie said. "You don't want to break it worse, do you?"

"What's the difference?" Christina wept. "Horses are the most important thing in my life, and I can't ride! And even if I could, I can't seem to ride my own horse. Obviously I'm basically useless as a human being. It would probably be much better for everyone if I weren't even around." She paused. "Maybe I should go to New York and live with your dad," she reflected.

"You wouldn't like it much," Melanie said. "He's never home, and the housekeeper hardly speaks any English. You can't go anywhere by yourself in the city, and you can only ride at Clarebrook. Your parents' place is so much better. You're lucky to have grown up with all this land, and grass and trees and horses," she added.

"How is it lucky if I can't even ride?" Christina said disgustedly.

"You're starting to sound like me," Melanie said. She came over and sat down on the edge of Christina's bed. "Listen, I was really unhappy when I first came here."

"No kidding," Christina said. "Nobody could even talk to you."

"I had a good reason to be unhappy," Melanie reminded her.

Christina knew what she meant. Melanie's mother, Mike's sister, had died when Melanie was little. Melanie had been raised by a series of nannies and housekeepers because her dad owned a record company and was too busy to spend much time with his daughter. Melanie was always getting into some kind of trouble. The last straw had been when she and a friend sneaked into Clarebrook, the city stable where she rode, took two horses out, and went riding in Central Park at night. On the way back, Melanie's horse had been hit by a cab and killed. After that incident Melanie's father sent her to live with Christina and her parents.

At first Christina had found Melanie impossible to get along with. But eventually Melanie took an interest in one of the Reeses' racehorses. The three-year-old black colt, Pirate Treasure, had been one of Whitebrook's most promising racers until he was injured in a race at Keeneland. While Pirate was still recovering, Melanie discovered that the colt was blind and could never race again. But now Pirate was working beautifully as a track pony—one of the horses who accompanied the racehorses to the starting gate, or to and from the training track. Ashleigh and Mike had promised to give the horse to Melanie if she behaved responsibly and stayed out of trouble. But as far as everyone was concerned, he pretty much already belonged to her.

Christina had noticed that since Melanie had become a "pony girl," she was like a different person. She was still tough and sarcastic sometimes, but she was much easier to talk to, and she didn't seem angry all the time, the way she had been when she first came to Whitebrook. Christina had discovered that she even liked having Melanie around—sometimes.

Melanie was peering at Christina intently. She had large brown eyes with a slight downward tilt that always made her look a little sad. With her petite features and white-blond hair, sometimes Melanie reminded Christina of an elf or a fairy—especially when Melanie had streaked her hair with blue Kool-Aid.

"What?" Christina said. "Why are you looking at me like that?"

"Well, I know you don't want Cassidy to ride Sterling. I wouldn't, either, if I were you. But I know you're going to have a hard time getting anyone else to do it. So. Do you think I could ride Sterling for you?" Melanie asked.

CHRISTINA SAT UP. SHE HADN'T THOUGHT ABOUT MELANIE riding Sterling. The idea startled her out of her tears. "I—I don't know," she stammered. "Do you think you can?"

Melanie had been riding only since she was about ten. She was pretty good for someone with so few years of experience, but Christina wasn't sure she was good enough to handle Sterling.

Melanie just gave her a cool look. "Thanks for the vote of confidence. I can try, can't I?" she asked, and added airily, "I don't see what else you can do, unless you plan to ask Cassidy after all." She stared at Christina and waited for an answer.

"I didn't mean that you're not a good rider," Christina said hastily. "It's just that—well, you know how Sterling is."

Melanie shrugged. "Yeah, so?"

"So do you think you can handle her? She can get quick sometimes—"

"No kidding," Melanie said.

"And you saw how she acted today. At the fences. Do you think you can deal with that?" Christina asked.

Melanie nodded. "I'm not afraid," she said confidently.

Christina wasn't sure if Melanie was telling the truth or not, but she *sounded* convincing. Maybe it would work. After all, Melanie didn't have to jump Sterling, she just had to keep her exercised.

"You know what? That's not a bad idea," Christina said. "Let's try it."

Melanie smiled. "I have an even better idea."

"What is it?" Christina asked.

"Well, assuming everything goes okay and I can handle Sterling, I'll keep on with her event training. Then you can still ride her in the event at Foxwood," Melanie said.

"But how?" Christina asked. "I can't use my arm properly." She gestured to the cast. "I won't be able to steer or stop like this. Besides, Mom and Dad would never let me ride with my arm in a cast."

"When's the event?" Melanie said impatiently.

"Two weeks from Saturday," Christina said.

"And what day is this?" Melanie demanded.

"Monday."

"And when do you get this big cast taken off?" Melanie prompted.

"The doctor said in two wee—" Christina broke off and began to smile. "I'll just have a small brace on my wrist then! I bet I can ride with that!" she exclaimed.

"Of course you can," Melanie said. "And you'll have almost a week to practice with it before the event. You'll definitely be ready by then. So you can tell Cassidy and Dylan you won't be needing any replacement team member."

Christina smiled broadly at her cousin. "Mel," she said, "you're a genius." She put her good arm around Melanie and gave her half a bear hug.

Melanie let herself be hugged for exactly three seconds, then wiggled out of Christina's hold and stood up. She put her hands on her hips and looked very businesslike. "Okay. So I'll meet you at the training barn at about nine o'clock, when I get done with Pirate," she said.

"I'll be there," Christina said. "Actually, maybe I'll come down early and watch some of the workouts," she said. "I haven't done that in a long time."

"Whatever," Melanie said with a shrug. She yawned. "I'm wiped out. I'm going to bed. What time is it, anyway?"

Christina leaned over and looked at the clock beside her bed. "Eight forty," she said.

Melanie laughed. "Man, if my friends in New York

knew I was going to bed so early all the time, I'd never hear the end of it."

"Well, when you get up at five thirty in the morning, you get tired earlier at night," Christina pointed out.

"Why do horses have to get up so early?" Melanie asked. "Couldn't we teach them to sleep in?"

Christina laughed at that. "Mel, if anyone can figure out a way to make horses sleep late, I bet you can. And tell me when you do," she added.

"You'll be the first to know," Melanie promised. "This living in the country is amazing," she muttered, heading down the hall to her room.

Christina felt much happier. The idea of Melanie exercising Sterling was beginning to sound better and better. Christina could stay close by while Melanie was on Sterling, and coach her if she needed it. She could also teach Melanie certain things Sterling liked and didn't like—special things Christina had gotten to know about the horse from riding her so much. And best of all, Melanie would keep Sterling in shape; Christina would almost certainly be able to ride in the event after all!

She got ready for bed, feeling happy for the first time since the morning. She hadn't forgotten about Dylan going out with Cassidy, but it seemed much easier to think about now that she didn't feel as though her whole life was ruined. Christina said good night to her parents and got into bed, carefully arranging a couple of pillows under her arm. She fell asleep thinking of galloping Sterling over the cross-country course at Foxwood Acres.

Early in the morning, Christina opened her eyes. Sunlight shone through the curtains and fell in a lacy pattern across the wooden floor. The clock beside her bed told her it was nearly seven o'clock. She had slept late. Melanie would already be down at the training oval. Christina got out of bed and almost put on her jodhpurs before she remembered that she wasn't going to be riding that day. With one arm she awkwardly pulled a T-shirt over her head, and then she chose a pair of shorts with an elastic waist so she wouldn't have to fool with buttons or zippers. She couldn't put her hair in a ponytail with one hand, so she raked a brush through it, tucked it behind her ears, and trotted down the stairs.

The kitchen was empty. Christina knew her parents were already out at work on the farm. Her dad would probably be in the barn office doing paperwork, and her mom would be riding horses or overseeing the workouts with Ian McLean. Christina gulped a glass of orange juice, grabbed a banana, and bounded out the door. She hurried out the backyard gate and down the hill to the training oval, feeling a little guilty for being the last one up and out.

"Good morning, Sleeping Beauty," Ashleigh said

as she jogged a horse along the rail of the training track.

"Morning, Mom," Christina said, approaching the rail. "How's Matilda today?"

Matilda was the gorgeous black filly Ashleigh was working with. "She's fine," Ashleigh said, pulling up. The three-year-old filly danced impatiently, and Ashleigh soothed her with a pat on her slender neck. "I'm surprised you recognized her," she added. "It's been so long since you've come down to watch the workouts."

"I know," Christina said. Wistfully she thought about trotting Sterling up and down the hilly pastures and through the woods, conditioning her for the event. That was what she'd usually be doing at this hour of the morning.

"What brings you down here this morning?" Ashleigh asked. "Don't tell me you've decided you're interested in racing after all."

Christina shook her head. "It's not that I don't appreciate Thoroughbred racing, Mom," she said. "It's a great sport. It's just that I like jumping and combined training so much better. Anyway, since I can't ride, I've got to be around horses somehow. So I promised Melanie I'd come see her and Pirate this morning."

"Wonderful," Ashleigh said. "You and your cousin seem to be getting along much better these days," she observed.

"Well, she's a whole lot easier to take now that she's got Pirate to work with," Christina said. "Where is she?"

"Over there." Ashleigh indicated the direction with a tilt of her head. Matilda snorted as if to say, *Hey, let's get going,* and Ashleigh moved off, jogging the filly around the outside rail.

Christina looked down the track for Melanie and spotted Pirate's black hindquarters and tail moving calmly down the track next to an antsy chestnut. She shaded her eyes with her good hand and tried to make out who the other horse was. But it wasn't until the horse reached the starting pole and galloped away that she recognized her.

The horse was Leap of Faith, a four-year-old chestnut who had always been a favorite of Christina's. Before she had Sterling, she had gone by Faith's stall nearly every day to give the filly a carrot or an apple. She tried to remember the last time she'd been to visit the other horses and realized guiltily that it had been a couple of months. Well, at least she'd have time to go see them now that she was "grounded."

Faith started around the turn then, and Christina recognized the rider's blue and white helmet cover. Sixteen-year-old Naomi Traeger was one of the apprentice jockeys at Whitebrook. Her older brother, Nathan, was a jockey who also rode the Reeses' horses. As Faith galloped gracefully around the turn and straightened toward the homestretch, Naomi bent lower, leaning into the horse's neck, and pushed the reins at Faith's head, signaling the filly to put on some speed.

The pair breezed down the homestretch. Faith's dainty head with her pretty white star bobbed in front of Naomi's face as they streaked past Christina. She watched them cross the finish and then come back to a slow gallop. Christina had seen a look of keen excitement on Naomi's face as they flew by. Faith's face was a study in determination when she ran, and as she jogged afterward it was clear from the proud arch of her neck and the relaxed snorts she let out that she had enjoyed the run as much as Naomi.

Though she had never wanted to ride racehorses, Christina had no trouble understanding how someone could be as passionate about racing as she herself was about combined training. After all, she reflected, riding a cross-country course was kind of a race, although you could get penalized for going too fast. And riding a jumper course was definitely a race against the clock.

"Hi," Melanie said, riding up on Pirate.

"Hi," Christina responded. "Hi, Pirate," she said, reaching out to stroke the huge gelding's muscular shoulder.

"He's so happy now that he's back on the track," Melanie said, patting him affectionately. "Aren't you, Pirate?"

Christina looked the horse over from head to tail. Though she liked gray horses best, Christina had to admit Pirate Treasure was a beautiful animal. His coat was all black, so dark and shiny that in places it glinted blue in the morning light. Except for the ugly, jagged scar on his chest where he'd gashed himself when he ran through the rail at Keeneland, the horse looked fit and healthy. The expression on his face was relaxed and expectant as he stood patiently waiting for Melanie to tell him what to do next. And although the vet said he could probably see only a hint of light and shadow, his brown eyes were large and kind.

"He sure looks better," Christina agreed.

Pirate had been an outstanding racer before he lost his sight to a degenerative eye disease called moon blindness. And he had seemed to love to run as much as a horse could. But after his accident at Keeneland, while he was turned out for several weeks, he became skinny and depressed. When Melanie began riding him, Christina had noticed that the horse began to perk up every time her cousin came near the track. Pirate would come out of his head-down, ambling gait and suddenly become animated again, stepping along in a lively walk and sometimes calling out in a hopeful whinny to his old racing mates.

If it hadn't been for Pirate, Christina reflected, Melanie might never have ridden a horse again. And if it hadn't been for Melanie, Pirate's future would have been grim. But the two had been strangely drawn to each other from the first day they met, and eventually each had helped the other to heal. Ponying racehorses around the track, Pirate and Melanie were as happy as could be.

"We have to pony Shining Moment to the starting gate and then I'm all finished," Melanie told Christina. "So as soon as I finish taking care of Pirate we can go over to Mona's."

"Great," Christina said.

Melanie glanced over and saw Anna Simms, one of the exercise riders, up on a strawberry roan colt with four black stockings named Shining Moment. The colt looked just like his dam, Shining, one of the best broodmares at Whitebrook. Shining belonged to Samantha McLean, Kevin's older sister, who was married and lived in Ireland.

"Melanie, I need you," Anna called. Shining Moment was stepping anxiously all over the place.

"Coming." Melanie gave her a wave. "See you in a little while," she said to Christina. "Let's go, Pirate."

Christina watched Melanie trot Pirate over to Anna and Shining Moment. Almost as soon as Pirate reached the colt's side, Shining Moment calmed down and began walking placidly toward the gate. And although he was excited to be on the track, Pirate seemed content just to be surrounded by racehorses. When he himself had been racing, his behavior sometimes had been erratic. But as a pony horse, he never seemed agitated by other horses bucking or acting up. As much as Pirate enjoyed his job, he took it seriously. He walked serenely along with his high-strung partners, escorting them all over the track and to and from the barns.

Watching Pirate and Melanie stand by while Shining Moment was loaded into the starting gate, Christina thought, *They're really good at this.* She was glad for her cousin, but at the same time she felt a little sad. She couldn't help wondering: Were she and Sterling as good a team?

When Melanie had finished her work, groomed Pirate, fed him, and put him away, the two girls headed across the pasture toward Gardener Farms. They hiked over the hill and around the trees before coming upon the fence that separated Mona's back pasture from Whitebrook Farm's pasture. Melanie opened the gate and then closed it behind them.

Christina could see the stables as soon as they were on the other side of the fence. She and Melanie had been ambling along, enjoying the sights and smells of a Kentucky farm in summer. But with the barn in sight, she began to walk faster, anxious to see her horse again. It had been less than twenty-four hours since she'd seen Sterling, but it felt more like a week.

"Hey, what's the rush?" Melanie grumbled.

"I just want to see Sterling," Christina explained.

They entered the cool shade of the stables, and Christina took a deep whiff of the familiar sweet yet salty musk of leather and hay and horses. For a second she closed her eyes and simply breathed it in. She couldn't live without it, she knew. Horses to Christina were the same as air and water.

"Where is she?" Melanie asked.

"I'm not sure," Christina said. Then she spotted Matt Lauery, the head groom, in the wash stall scrubbing water buckets, and went to ask him.

"Um, Matt?" Christina said. She was a little intimidated by him, but she could never figure out exactly why. Matt always sounded to Christina like he was about to snap at her, though he never had.

Matt was sitting on one upside-down bucket while he scrubbed at another. He glanced at Christina and Melanie but kept working. "What do you want?" he asked.

"Do you know where my horse is, Sterling Dream?" Christina asked.

Matt's dark head was still bent over the bucket he was scrubbing. "Yep," he said. He held the bucket up and looked at it critically.

Christina waited for him to tell her where her horse was, but he simply set the bucket aside and reached for another. She exchanged a quick glance with Melanie, who rolled her eyes.

"Well, where is she?" Melanie demanded.

Christina looked at her cousin admiringly. Melanie wasn't afraid to talk to anyone. Sometimes Christina wished she were that bold.

Matt looked around at Melanie. Christina cringed, expecting him to scold her or something, but he just said, "She's in that second stall by the front door, where Zan used to be."

"Thanks," Melanie said, heading up the barn aisle.

Matt nodded and turned back to his buckets.

"Thanks," Christina echoed her cousin, and followed her up the aisle.

The nameplate on the stall still said Zanzibar, although the horse inside was definitely Sterling. Zan had been sold recently to a woman from California. Mona's reputation as an excellent horse trainer extended far beyond Kentucky. Christina knew that Mona had even sold horses to customers from Europe.

An index card had been stapled to the stall, with Sterling's name handwritten on it in black marker along with instructions for feeding and turnout. The horse was looking out the window of the stall when Christina approached, but when the mare heard the click and slide of the latch on her door, she turned around to see who was opening her stall.

"Hi, Sterling," Christina crooned in the special voice she used to talk to her horse.

Sterling stepped toward Christina and nickered softly.

"Hi, pretty girl," Christina murmured, reaching into her pocket for a peppermint. She unwrapped it, giggling as the mare heard the candy wrapper crackle and began searching eagerly for the treat. "Here you go," she said, holding the peppermint under Sterling's muzzle.

Sterling lipped the treat and crunched it happily. Christina stroked the mare's sleek dapple gray neck. Then she closed her eyes and rested her cheek against Sterling's neck, loving the feel of her soft coat and the smell of the horse's warm, peppermint breath.

"Let's get going." Melanie's voice interrupted Christina's horse reverie. "Where's your tack?"

Christina opened her eyes. Melanie was standing in the doorway of the stall in her typical hands-on-hips, businesslike stance. "In the tack room," Christina said, as if Melanie should know that.

"Well, where's the tack room?" Melanie demanded. "I've never ridden here before, remember?"

"Oh. Sorry," Christina said. She pointed to the right door, and Melanie went to get Christina's saddle and bridle. In a minute she was back, lugging the saddle, the bridle slung over her shoulder.

"Just put them right there for now," Christina told her, pointing to a saddle rack and a bridle hook outside Sterling's stall. Christina brought Sterling out into the aisle and put her in the crossties. Then she found a hoof pick and started to clean Sterling's feet. Melanie grabbed a rubber currycomb and was about to start currying Sterling's neck when Christina stopped her.

"What are you doing?" Christina asked.

"I'm helping you groom her," Melanie said. "What does it look like I'm doing?" She started for Sterling's neck again with the currycomb, and again Christina stopped her.

"Sterling doesn't like to be touched by just anybody," Christina said. "Remember, she was abused at the track."

Melanie gave her cousin an exasperated look. "How am I supposed to ride her if I can't even touch her?" she exclaimed.

Christina opened her mouth to protest, but then she closed it again. Melanie was right, she realized. "Just be careful," she warned. "She'll still bite sometimes if you move suddenly or startle her somehow."

"Yeah, yeah," Melanie said, moving the currycomb in a circular motion over the horse's body.

Christina bent to pick up Sterling's foot and stopped. "Actually, why don't I curry her and you pick out her feet? I just realized, I can't do it with one arm," she said sheepishly.

Melanie gave her an I-told-you-so look and traded the currycomb for the hoof pick. Working together, the two girls soon had the horse groomed and tacked. Christina started to lead her out the barn door, then stopped.

"Here," she said, handing Melanie the reins. "I guess you should lead her."

They headed down to the arena, Melanie leading Sterling and Christina walking beside her. Christina looked around for Mona but was relieved that she wasn't around. Maybe she had gone to town. Or maybe she was riding one of her horses cross-country. Anyway, if Melanie couldn't handle Sterling, Christina thought, it would be better if Mona didn't know about it.

"Think you can give me a leg up?" Melanie asked.

"Sure," Christina said.

Melanie faced the saddle and gathered up the reins in her left hand. She bent her left knee; Christina took hold of it with her good arm and boosted her cousin onto the horse. Christina watched while Melanie shortened the stirrups and untwisted the reins. She had thought that this was going to work, but now she wasn't so sure. She knew what a handful Sterling could be at times. And Melanie looked so tiny high up on Sterling.

"Well, here we go," Melanie said cheerfully.

"I sure hope this works," Christina said doubtfully, watching Melanie and Sterling begin to walk around the arena.

# 7

AFTER WALKING AROUND THE RING A FEW TIMES, MELANIE asked Sterling to pick up a trot, and Christina held her breath. She stood in the center of the arena, where Mona usually stood, and watched as someone else rode her horse around the ring. Part of her hoped Sterling would be on her best behavior with Melanie. She really wanted this to work out.

But deep inside her was another part that hoped Sterling would misbehave. Then at least Christina could blame the accident with Sterling on the horse's behavior, instead of feeling that it was her own riding that had caused the fall.

She watched Melanie critically but could find nothing wrong with the girl's riding. Melanie was staying light in her seat and soft in her hand with Sterling, just as Christina had instructed her, and

Sterling was trotting around like an angel, looking as relaxed as she had with Mona the day before.

For a second Christina felt jealous that her cousin seemed to be handling Sterling so well. But then she pushed it aside. *You want this to work, remember?* she scolded herself. Christina knew the only way she would be able to ride in the event would be to have someone keep working with Sterling. And if Melanie couldn't do it, there was no one else. *Unless you let Cassidy ride her,* a tiny voice in her head reminded her.

"No way," Christina said aloud.

"What?" Melanie said, trotting by.

"Nothing," Christina said. "How are you doing?" she asked anxiously.

"Fine, I think," Melanie said. "How do we look?"

"You look pretty good," Christina admitted. "Want to try a canter?"

"Sure," Melanie said. She walked Sterling for a moment, then broke into a canter, moving smoothly and quietly around the arena. Christina felt as if she were taking every stride along with Melanie. When Melanie brought Sterling down to a walk, Christina relaxed. She felt exhausted and then realized she'd been holding her breath. She let it out and breathed deeply.

"Good girl," Melanie said, rewarding Sterling with a pat and giving her a long rein. "Wow, she has a great canter."

"I know," Christina said, wishing she could be

enjoying her own horse's canter instead of watching Melanie enjoy it. She went over and began walking along beside Sterling's shoulder.

"I think we're going to be fine," Melanie said.

Christina began to smile. "I think you're right," she said. "It looks like I'm going to get to ride in the event after all."

Melanie put the reins in one hand and held out her other hand to Christina, palm out. "Give it up," she said with a grin. "You're all over that event."

Christina slapped her own hand on top of her cousin's in a triumphant high five.

Later, when they had put Sterling away, Mona came into the barn leading one of the young horses she was training. She had been riding out in the pasture, just as Christina had guessed. "Hi, girls," Mona said, looking surprised to see them.

"Hi, Mona," Christina said cheerfully. "How's Sebastian?" She went over to the big gray three-year-old Mona had been riding and began scratching his withers.

"Oh, he's coming along," Mona said, smiling as Sebastian leaned into Christina's hand, urging her to scratch harder. "He likes that," she commented. "By the way, did you find someone to ride Sterling for you?" she asked casually, undoing Sebastian's girth. She went around to his off side and laid the girth across the saddle, then lifted it off his back.

"Yes," Christina said.

"Hold him for me for a sec, will you?" Mona said.

"I got him." Christina took Sebastian's reins while Mona went into the tack room with her saddle.

When she came out, Mona said, "So who did you get?"

Christina paused, then answered, "Melanie."

"Really?" Mona said. She glanced over at Melanie, who simply met Mona's look with an impenetrable stare.

Christina wished she could look people unflinchingly in the eye the way Melanie could. She knew what Mona was wondering: Was Melanie experienced enough to handle Sterling? But she also knew that Mona had never seen Melanie ride, so she couldn't really say anything about it.

"She rode her this morning, and they got along great," Christina volunteered. "Sterling really seemed to like her. I think it'll work out fine."

"Good," Mona said in a politely encouraging way. "Well, I'm glad you found someone to take care of her for you. How's your wrist today?"

"Oh, it doesn't really bother me much," Christina said. "The cast is the worst part. It's itchy, and my arm feels all stiff, like it wants to be straight."

"Well, it'll be off before you know it," Mona said. She took Sebastian's reins from Christina and led him up the aisle. "Matt, can you take Sebastian, please? I've got to get on Serendipity before Martha comes." She glanced at her watch as Matt took Sebastian from her. "And don't forget to clean Geraldo's sheath," she reminded him.

"Sarah's going to do it," Matt said.

Sarah was a university student who worked for Mona. She was a part-time groom who also taught beginner lessons. Mona shook her head. "I want you to do it," she told Matt. "Geraldo's fussy, and Sarah's inexperienced. I don't want her getting kicked."

Christina heard someone come into the barn as she watched Matt lead Sebastian away. She turned around and saw Dylan, carrying a saddle in a blue bag sporting a stylish monogram that read *CNS*.

"Hi, Dylan," Christina chirped.

"Hi," he said.

"Whose saddle is that?" she asked curiously.

"Cassidy's," Dylan said. "I'm helping her move her stuff in."

"Oh," Christina said, sorry she'd asked.

Then Cassidy came into the barn, carrying a grooming kit and wearing a bridle over each shoulder.

"Hi, Christina," she said. "How's the wrist?"

"Fine," Christina said flatly.

Cassidy stopped and shifted her stance so that she could rest the grooming kit on her thigh for a moment. "Listen, I told Mona I'd be happy to exercise Sterling for you until your wrist gets better," she said.

"I already found someone to exercise her,"

Christina said. *How could Cassidy have the nerve to go to a movie with Dylan and then act like nothing has happened?* she wondered furiously.

"Oh? Who?" Cassidy asked.

"Me," Melanie said.

"Oh, I didn't know you rode," Cassidy said.

"I didn't know you had a brain," Melanie said sweetly.

Christina almost laughed out loud. Cassidy gave Melanie a strange look, then ignored her and turned back to Christina. "Anyway, I think she's a really sweet little horse, and I'll be glad to help you out with her any time," she offered.

"Melanie's got it covered," Christina said coolly. "But thanks anyway."

"No problem," Cassidy said.

"By the way," Christina said, "Dylan told me you were planning to take my place on the show team."

"Oh, yeah, I said I would ride so they wouldn't have to scratch the team entry. It would be such a shame for Dylan and Katie not to ride, after all the hard work they've put in training for the event," Cassidy said.

*What about all my hard work?* Christina thought. She said, "Well, I don't need anyone to take my place. I'm still going to compete in the event."

Cassidy gave her a skeptical look. "How? Your arm's in a cast," she pointed out.

"I get it off before the event," Christina said. "And

Melanie's going to keep Sterling exercised for me. So I'll be able to ride. We won't be needing you."

Cassidy regarded her for a moment, then turned without a word. "Dylan?" she said, looking around. "Where are you?"

"In here," he answered from the tack room. "Come show me where you want this stuff."

"Coming," Cassidy said, lugging the grooming kit in the direction of the tack room.

"I'll be glad to help you out with your sweet little horse," Melanie mimicked Cassidy when she was out of sight. She made a face. "She acts like she's Mona or something. Who does she think she is?"

"I don't think she liked it when I told her she wasn't riding on the team," Christina said.

"No kidding." Melanie chuckled.

"I can't believe you asked her if she had a brain," Christina said, giggling. Then she looked seriously at her cousin. "Hey, thanks for being on my side," she said. "Right now I feel like you're the only one who is."

"What are cousins for?" Melanie said.

The next day Melanie rode Sterling again, and the two seemed to get along even better. Christina coached her cousin through the training-level dressage test Sterling would be performing at the event. They had to ride through a certain pattern at a walk, trot, and canter, demonstrating circles and straight lines. There were dressage letters placed around the arena: A, K, E, H, C, M, B, F, and the imaginary letter X at the center of the arena. The test called for the rider to execute certain commands at each letter. And except for the halts at the beginning and end of the test, Melanie rode through it almost as well as Christina could.

"I always thought halts were the easiest," Melanie said. "How come I'm having such a hard time keeping her straight?"

"Halts look easy," Christina said, "but actually they're pretty difficult to do correctly. Sterling always wants to wiggle her hindquarters to the left just when you think you've got her halted nicely. Mona makes me work and work on them, so I've gotten to where I can usually keep her straight."

"You're right," Melanie said. "Let me try it again." She picked up a trot and circled the ring.

"Sterling's a genius at avoiding halting square," Christina called as she followed Melanie and Sterling with her eyes. "I'll think I have a perfect halt, and then she'll scoot her hind end over sideways just as I'm putting my reins into one hand to salute the judge."

Melanie trotted Sterling up the center line and aimed for X. Christina watched her ask Sterling to halt. "Now be ready," Christina warned. "Keep your left leg back a little and be ready to push against her to keep her from shifting her hindquarters."

Melanie placed the reins into her left hand and made a quick salute to an imaginary judge. This time she managed to keep Sterling still and straight. She let the horse walk out of the halt and patted her neck.

"Well, that was better," Christina commented.

"The left leg thing worked," Melanie said. "I think when I get to know her I'll be able to ride her even better."

"You definitely will," Christina agreed.

"Let's try jumping her," Melanie suggested.

"Oh, we can't," Christina said. "No one's allowed to jump alone."

"I'm not alone," Melanie said. "You're here."

Christina looked around uneasily. Mona was out riding Sebastian again, somewhere in the pasture. Christina had always assumed that the farm rule against jumping alone meant jumping without an instructor around. Did they dare jump Sterling without Mona?

"What about it?" Melanie asked.

"I don't know," Christina said hesitantly. "I'm not sure it's a good idea to jump without Mona here."

"Why not? Sterling's your horse, isn't she?" Melanie persisted. "We've got to keep her working over fences or she won't be ready for the event, right?"

"Right, but—"

"Well, then," Melanie cut her off, "let's do it."

"But Sterling hasn't jumped since—since Monday,"

Christina pointed out. "And you saw how she was behaving then. What if she's still acting up today? Do you really think we should try jumping her without Mona?"

"I'm not afraid," Melanie said. "And I'm the one riding her. Besides, back at Whitebrook you wouldn't have to have permission."

Christina looked around. There was a crossrail leading to a small vertical, set at less than two feet. "Okay . . . I guess. Try the crossrail to the vertical," she suggested.

"No, I thought I'd start with the liverpool," Melanie said sarcastically.

"Oh, no, don't do that!" Christina said, looking at her cousin with alarm.

"Christina!" Melanie looked at her incredulously. "I'm kidding, okay?"

"Oh," Christina said, relieved.

"The girl has no sense of humor," Melanie muttered.

"Yes, I do," Christina argued. "I'm just worried, that's all."

"Relax, then," Melanie said. "It's no wonder Sterling freaked out on you. You'd make anyone nervous."

Christina stared at the dirt. So everyone did think the accident was her fault. She knew Melanie hadn't meant to hurt her feelings, but the remark had stung. She felt tears beginning to burn behind her eyes.

"Hey, I didn't mean that the way it sounded," Melanie said, as gently as Melanie ever said anything.

"That's okay," Christina said, keeping her eyes on the crossrail so Melanie wouldn't see tears shining in them. "Well, what are you waiting for? Go on and jump her."

"I am, but . . . don't you think I should carry a crop?" Melanie asked.

"No!" Christina said, forgetting to feel sorry for herself. "Didn't you see what happened when I used the crop on her?"

"It wasn't the crop that made her bolt," Melanie pointed out. "She landed in the water and stumbled getting out. That spooked her."

"It was the crop," Christina insisted. "I never should have used it on her, no matter what anyone said. When I rescued her from Belmont I promised her no one would ever hit her again. I can't believe I was the one who broke that promise." Christina looked at her horse, her eyes blurring with tears all over again. "She'll probably never forgive me," she sniffed.

"Christina, she's a horse," Melanie said impatiently. "I doubt she even remembers that you hit her."

"I'll bet you she does," Christina said.

"Anyway, it's not you riding her, it's me," Melanie said. "I've only jumped the school horses at Clarebrook. They try to refuse and run out at jumps all the time, so I'm used to that. But I would feel much better if I had a stick. Maybe I won't need to use it on her," Melanie suggested hopefully. "Maybe just carrying it is enough."

"No," Christina said stubbornly. "If you can't do it without hitting her, I won't let you ride her." She crossed her arms and looked at Melanie.

Melanie sighed. "I'm doing this for *you*, remember?" she said, sounding exasperated.

"Then do it the way I say," Christina said.

"Okay," Melanie said doubtfully.

Christina watched as Melanie went into a trot and started toward the crossrail. Melanie got into two-point position a little early, and Christina thought maybe Sterling would run out, but she didn't. The horse picked up her front legs and neatly cleared the little crossrail. Then Melanie cantered down over the vertical and around the turn.

"How was that?" she called.

"Good," Christina said. "Try it again."

Melanie jumped Sterling down the line again. Christina thought it looked even smoother than the first time.

"How high will you have to jump in the cross-country course?" Melanie asked.

"The maximum height at the novice level is two feet eleven inches," Christina said. "But Mona told me most of the fences will probably be lower than that."

"I can jump two feet six inches," Melanie said. "Put the jumps up to that and let me try her over them."

"Do you think we ought to?" Christina asked. "I mean, she just did that so well, maybe we should end on a good note today."

"I only jumped four jumps, and they're little-bitty ones," Melanie said. "Let's get real here. If she's going to be ready for the event, we'd better work on the problems now, if there are any."

"I guess you're right," Christina said. Melanie had Sterling jumping nicely. Christina was curious to see how the mare would jump over a slightly higher fence. "Okay," she decided. "I'm going to leave the crossrail, but I'll raise the vertical to two feet three inches. Then if she's fine over that, I'll raise it to two feet six inches."

"Okay," Melanie said. She waited while Christina raised the top rail of the vertical. Then she came at the crossrail again. Sterling jumped both fences flawlessly. Melanie patted the horse. "Raise 'em," she ordered Christina.

Christina set the rail higher and stepped back. She thought Melanie might have trouble now that the fence was almost a foot taller, but again Sterling cleared the two jumps as if they were nothing.

"How'd that look?" Melanie asked.

"Great," Christina said, still a little amazed.

"Put it up to two-nine," Melanie said.

"But I thought you only jumped two-six," Christina said.

"So far I've only jumped two-six. Today I'm going to jump two-nine," Melanie said confidently.

"Are you sure?" Christina asked. She didn't feel at all confident. Raising the height of jumps for a rider was an instructor's job. Christina wasn't sure if Melanie was ready for two feet nine inches or not, and she didn't feel qualified to judge.

"It's only three more inches," Melanie said pragmatically. "How different can it be?"

"Okay," Christina said. "But we're not raising them any more than that."

"Whatever," Melanie said, shrugging. She rested her hands on Sterling's withers and looked indifferently off toward the barn while Christina set the fence up three more inches. When it was done, Melanie shortened the reins and asked Sterling to canter.

Christina watched them come around the turn and straighten out to approach the crossrail. Sterling's black legs stroked the ground gracefully with every stride, and her unusual silver-streaked mane blew back, showing off the elegant curve of her neck. *What a gorgeous horse,* Christina thought proudly. *And she's mine.*

She couldn't stop a smile from breaking over her face as Sterling cleared the crossrail. She watched the horse land lightly on the other side and start for the next jump, where the vertical was set at two feet nine inches. Sterling seemed to notice the jump was set higher, and quickened her pace a little. Christina crossed her fingers and held her breath again as they reached the jump.

Sterling rocked back on her haunches and soared over it. But the horse had to make more of a jumping effort to get over the higher fence. Though Melanie was in jumping position, her legs swung back, tipping her a little too far forward and causing her to lose her position over the saddle. Christina cringed as Sterling hit the ground on the other side of the jump and Melanie landed sloppily on her hands.

Christina closed her eyes for a second, afraid to look. But when she opened them she saw Melanie cantering away, looking pleased with herself. With a sigh of relief that nothing bad had happened, Christina waited for Melanie to bring Sterling down to a walk. That was enough jumping for one day, Christina decided. Somehow she'd have to break it to Melanie that she wasn't quite ready to jump two-nine.

She looked around, expecting to see Melanie and Sterling walking toward her. Instead she saw that they were still cantering.

"Melanie, that's enough for Sterling today," Christina called to her. "Let her walk, okay?"

But Melanie kept cantering.

"Melanie, walk," Christina said louder, in case she hadn't heard her the first time.

But Melanie still didn't walk. She kept cantering, then she turned toward one of the jumps at the end of the ring.

"What are you doing?" Christina asked, alarmed. In front of her cousin was the liverpool that Christina had tried to jump before. Christina looked at Melanie's face for a second. Was she kidding?

"Okay," Christina said. "You fooled me. Ha ha, very funny." She expected to see Melanie steer around the jump and come up laughing.

But Melanie's eyes were full of determination as she kept Sterling heading toward the water jump. Christina felt the blood drain from her own face as Melanie bent forward into two-point position and cantered straight toward the liverpool.

"MELANIE, NO!" CHRISTINA SHOUTED. "ARE YOU CRAZY?"

But Melanie ignored the warning. She was right at the fence.

"Oh, no," Christina said, feeling nauseous. Melanie was going to kill herself, on Christina's horse, right there in front of her. She couldn't watch.

But she couldn't look away, either. Melanie began pulling on the left rein. It looked like Sterling was trying to turn away from the water. Christina saw Melanie kick Sterling with her right leg and pull harder on the left rein to try and straighten her approach again.

"Melanie, don't! Oh, please don't," Christina whispered.

Then Sterling made up her own mind. Right in

front of the liverpool she suddenly darted to the right and ran past the jump.

Christina had one second to be relieved that Sterling hadn't jumped the liverpool and that Melanie had managed to stay on, probably because she'd been grabbing Sterling's mane as she came toward the jump. But in the next second her relief turned to terror as she realized that Sterling was running away with Melanie, and Melanie didn't seem to be doing anything to stop her.

"Oh, no," Christina gasped. "Omigosh, omigosh." She tried to think what to do. Then the galloping horse streaked past her as if she were back at the racetrack. Melanie was still hunched forward in what was left of her jumping position, and her face showed a kind of frozen amazement as they tore by.

"Melanie!" Christina yelled. "Stop her! Pull the reins! Sit up and pull the reins." Desperately she tried to figure out what Mona would tell her to do.

The answer came in someone else's voice. "Pulley rein!" someone yelled in a calm but strong voice that carried over the sound of Sterling's thundering hooves. "Put one hand on her neck, and sit up and yank the other rein as hard as you can."

Melanie obeyed. She set one hand against Sterling's neck and gave several sharp tugs upward and across her neck. Sterling's head shot up, and she checked her bolt almost instantly, throwing Melanie forward with the sudden stop.

"Thank goodness," Christina said. Then she looked around to see who it was who had remembered the pulley rein and helped Melanie.

Cassidy was walking toward them, a concerned expression on her face. "Are you okay?" she asked Melanie.

Christina moved toward Melanie and Sterling, intending to catch the horse and hold her. But in her excitement she forgot to approach the horse slowly and calmly. Sterling spooked at Christina and cantered away again.

"Oh, no," Christina wailed.

Melanie was still almost lying on Sterling's neck, gripping Sterling's shoulders with her knees. "Melanie, sit up," Christina called anxiously. Sterling was still cantering, but she might start to gallop again any second. If Melanie stayed on her neck like that, she would be sure to fall off.

"I can't," Melanie said.

Somehow she was tipped so far forward that she couldn't seem to get any leverage with her arms to push herself back into the saddle. Sterling was still cantering around, her ears flicking back and forth uneasily, as if she wasn't quite sure about this new style of riding. Christina figured it was only a matter of time before the horse decided to run away again and Melanie went flying off.

"Melanie, try to shorten the reins," Christina urged her.

"I can't," Melanie said as Sterling cantered past on her second lap around the arena.

"Jump off," Christina suggested.

But apparently Melanie couldn't do that, either. "Stop her," Melanie pleaded, struggling to hold on.

"I'm not riding her," Christina said, feeling helpless. "You've got to try to do something, Melanie. Sit up, or jump off." Christina tried to sound calm, but her panic was mounting. Sterling had sped up a little, and Melanie was looking more and more off balance.

"Christina, please stop her," Melanie begged as she cantered by for the third time.

Then, as Sterling began her fourth lap around the ring, Cassidy walked purposefully toward a corner and stopped about ten feet away from it, her eye on the cantering horse. *What's she doing?* Christina wondered.

As Sterling headed for the corner, Cassidy began to move closer to the track. When Sterling started to slow a little to make the turn, Cassidy reached out and caught her by the inside rein, which was flopping loosely about her neck.

"Whoa," Cassidy said. She pulled the rein firmly, slowing the horse and turning her away from the rail at the same time. She had to jog along with the horse for a few steps but soon had her stopped. Then she stood by the horse's side, patting her soothingly.

Relieved that the disaster had been averted,

Christina hurried to her horse, walking as fast as she dared. She didn't want to spook her again.

"Mel! Are you okay, Mel?" Christina asked.

Melanie nodded, panting. Her arms were trembling and she still held on around Sterling's neck.

"Maybe you should get off," Christina suggested.

Melanie slowly leaned over and lowered herself to the ground. She stood there shakily, looking dazed. Her cheeks were flushed and her eyes were two huge pools of fear in her small face. It was the first time Christina had ever seen her cousin look scared of anything.

"That was some bolt," Cassidy said.

"Wow" was all Melanie could say.

Christina looked at Sterling. The horse was sweaty and blowing from all the cantering. Her nostrils flared wide with each breath, showing pink inside them.

"You'd better get her cooled off," Cassidy said.

"I know," Christina snapped. She took the reins from Cassidy and started to lead Sterling toward the gate. She would take her up to the barn and hose her down.

"Here, let me loosen her girth," Cassidy offered.

"It's okay. I can do it," Christina muttered, struggling with the buckles.

"Let me do it," Cassidy said again. "I'll take her saddle up for you. It's got to be hard with that cast."

Christina was embarrassed that Cassidy had seen Sterling misbehave again. Worse, Cassidy had been the only one of the three who had seemed to know how to stop Sterling. Now Cassidy was reaching to undo the girth. "Let go," Christina said.

"I'm just trying to help," Cassidy said, drawing back.

"I don't need your help," Christina said icily. She started to lead Sterling away.

"Okay . . . ," Cassidy said doubtfully. "Whatever." She turned to Melanie. "Are you sure you're all right?"

"I—I didn't know she could go so fast," Melanie finally stammered. "That horse is crazy! Thanks for stopping her," she said gratefully.

*Crazy? How could she blame it on the horse?* Christina stopped and turned around. "You shouldn't have tried to jump the liverpool!" she snapped. "That was stupid and dangerous. You could have really gotten hurt!"

"I was trying to help you, remember?" Melanie said.

"I can do without that kind of help," Christina said. "And so can Sterling." She whirled and started across the ring again.

"Fine," Melanie said. "Then I'm sure you don't need me to exercise her anymore."

Christina stopped and turned around. "Melanie, that's not what I meant. I just don't think you should have tried to jump the liverpool with her. It's not that I don't want you to ride her."

"Too bad," Melanie said. "Find somebody else to ride your crazy horse for you." She stalked away toward the pasture gate.

Christina guessed she was headed back home. "Melanie!" she called after her. "Come on! Please don't leave."

Melanie gave her one scornful glance before she marched through the gate and closed it behind her. Christina could see by the set of her cousin's shoulders that she wasn't going to come back.

"Shoot!" Christina said. But she didn't have time to worry about Melanie. She had to get Sterling cooled off.

She glanced over at Cassidy, who had seen the whole exchange. Cassidy was looking at her with a mixture of pity and distaste. Christina gave her the most withering look she could manage and led Sterling away.

She got Sterling into the wash stall outside. It was awkward untacking her with one arm, but she managed to get the saddle off. She decided to worry about the halter later. She held the reins gingerly in her left hand and the hose in her right. She directed the spray on the horse's legs first, to get her used to it, then onto her chest and neck.

After a few moments under the cool water, Sterling had stopped blowing. She snorted and tossed her head, enjoying the refreshing shower. For a moment Christina actually forgot about her problems. It was too much fun taking care of her horse.

"Sterling, tell me something," Christina said, sending a fine spray at the horse's forehead, being careful not to squirt it into her ears. "How can a horse that hates rain and is afraid to put her feet in a puddle like to be drenched with a hose?"

Sterling stuck her face into the spray eagerly, with her eyes shut and her ears flat back to keep the water out of them. Christina laughed and lowered the hose, adjusting the spray to a finer one. Sterling opened her eyes and took the nozzle in her teeth, gulping the spray and making monkey faces with her lips as she sucked at the water.

Christina looked at her horse playing with the hose and tried to understand how she could love Sterling so much yet at the same time be so completely disappointed in her.

The next day Christina walked over to Gardener Farm alone. She was planning to talk to Melanie about riding Sterling again when she'd had a day or two to cool off. For now she was just going to turn Sterling out.

There were a couple of paddocks in which horses could be left to roam and graze. Christina went looking for Mona, to ask her which one she could put Sterling in. She poked her head in the barn first. Sebastian and Foster were both in their stalls. In fact, all of the horses Mona rode were in their stalls. But Mona was nowhere around. Then Christina heard Mona's teaching voice and realized she was down in the ring giving a lesson.

Christina started down the hill to ask Mona which paddock to use. The person having the lesson was trotting around on a gray horse, doing bending and leg-yielding exercises. Christina was so intent on Mona that at first she didn't really pay attention to the horse and rider.

"Mona?" Christina called.

Mona turned around. Christina was about to ask her the question when suddenly she realized that she knew the horse in the ring. And the rider.

The horse was Sterling. And Cassidy was riding her. Christina simply couldn't believe what she was seeing. And she knew that when she did believe it, she would be as angry as she had ever been.

"What are you doing?" Christina said.

Cassidy pulled up. "What do you mean? What's the matter?" she asked uneasily.

"What are you doing riding Sterling?" Christina demanded. "Who said you could ride my horse?"

"Chris, it's—" Mona began.

"Mona!" Christina said furiously. "Why is she riding my horse?"

"That's enough, Christina," Mona said. "If you stop yelling for a moment, I'll tell you."

"I never said she could ride my horse." Christina folded her arms and glared at Cassidy. "How dare you? You get off her right now—this instant!"

Cassidy started to swing out of the saddle. Christina fought a desire to pull the girl off the horse herself.

"Cassidy, wait," Mona said. "Christina, I called your house last night to ask permission, but you were already asleep. Ashleigh said it would be fine. She said she'd tell you about it this morning."

"I don't care what my mother said. Sterling's my horse, and I didn't give permission for anyone to ride her!" Christina insisted.

Mona was looking at her in disbelief. Cassidy looked back and forth between the two of them. Christina realized she probably sounded as though she was having a tantrum, but she was so angry she didn't care. "Get *off*," she hissed.

Cassidy started to dismount again, but Mona motioned for her to stay put. "I thought it would be a good idea to get Sterling jumping again right away. Cassidy's experienced enough to school her if she misbehaves," Mona explained. "I heard what happened yesterday," she added pointedly.

Cassidy had been looking more and more uncomfortable. "Mona, I'm getting off," Cassidy said. She dismounted and swiftly began to run up the stirrups. She loosened the girth and pulled her saddle off Sterling's back. Then she turned to Christina. "I'm sorry," she said. "I didn't know you didn't want anyone else riding her." She held out the reins to Christina. "Do you want me to put her away, or would you prefer to do it?"

Wordlessly Christina took the reins and stomped up the hill with her horse. Angrily she brushed the sweat marks from Sterling's back. *How could they?* she fumed. *How could they use my horse without asking?*

When her arm ached from brushing Sterling's back over and over, she finally put the brush away and put Sterling in her stall. Then she stalked home across the pasture.

On the way home, she had time to cool off a little. She realized that Mona and Cassidy had meant to be helpful, but she still thought that what they had done was wrong. By the time she got home it was her mother she was really angry with.

But when Christina confronted her mother, Ashleigh explained, "You were already asleep when Mona called. I'm sorry for going against your wishes, but I thought it was a good idea. You always take Mona's advice about training horses. I'm also sorry I didn't tell you this morning, but you were sleeping when I got up, and when I came back to the house after the workouts you had already left."

Christina still felt taken advantage of, but gradually her anger dissolved. She tried to forget about the incident and concentrated instead on figuring out a way to convince Melanie to ride Sterling again.

At dinner that night Christina avoided looking at Melanie. But when she did steal a glance at her she saw that Melanie, as usual, was completely unafraid to look her right in the eye. She tried meeting Melanie's stare for a few seconds, but she finally had to look away. Instead she studied her green beans and tried to decide what Melanie was thinking.

"May I be excused?" Melanie said.

"You may," Mike said.

Melanie took her plate, emptied the bits of leftover food into the compost bucket, and went upstairs.

Christina decided that this would be the best time to talk Melanie into riding Sterling again. "May I be excused, too?" she asked.

"You may," her dad said again.

Christina cleared her own plate, then scurried up the stairs after Melanie. She turned right at the top of the stairs and went to her cousin's room. The door was closed.

Christina paused for a moment. She hoped Melanie wasn't too mad. Then she knocked softly on the door.

"Who is it?" Melanie asked, her voice sounding muffled through the door.

"It's me," Christina said.

"What do you want?"

Christina sighed. "Can I come in, please?"

There was a pause. "I guess," Melanie said.

Christina opened the door. Melanie was sitting at her desk with a sketch pad before her. She loved to draw and was actually very talented. Christina knew that because she had sneaked a look in her sketchbook once, while Melanie was out riding Pirate. She had to sneak; she'd been dying of curiosity, and Melanie would never voluntarily show her drawings to anyone.

This time, when Christina came into the room, Melanie snapped her sketchbook closed, as usual, and kept a protective hand over it.

"Hi," Christina said tentatively.

"Hi," Melanie echoed.

"Can I see?" Christina asked, gesturing toward the sketchbook.

She expected the usual negative response, and was surprised when Melanie slowly opened the book to the page she'd been drawing on and shifted herself a little to one side, inviting Christina to look. Christina stepped closer and took a look at the drawing.

"It's Sterling!" Christina said. The likeness was amazing, the shading and detail very sophisticated. "Melanie, that's beautiful!" she said admiringly. "I wish I could draw like that."

Melanie pretended to be indifferent, but Christina thought she looked slightly pleased. "Here," Melanie said. She tore the page out of the book and handed it to Christina. "You can have it."

"Really?" Christina asked, genuinely pleased. "I can keep it?"

"I was going to give it to you anyway," Melanie said.

Christina let her eyes move over the drawing. The ebony pencil showed the darks and lights of the mare's coloring and brought out the lines and curves of her muscles and bones in a startlingly realistic way. The horse was standing in a paddock with one front foot poised as if she were about to walk away, her head looking forward as if she'd been grazing and something had just caught her attention. The silhouette of her neck and back and the shape of her face and pricked ears were Sterling's exactly.

"Melanie, this is amazing," Christina said, staring at the drawing. "This is *so* good. I mean, you should be an artist."

"I *am* an artist," Melanie observed.

"I mean—you know what I mean. You should have a show or something," Christina said.

"One day I will," Melanie said. "It's a good thing I can draw—I sure don't have much of a future as a rider."

"That's not true," Christina objected. "You're a great rider. Especially when you're at the track, ponying with Pirate."

"I'm an *okay* rider," Melanie said. "I'm not talented, like you or Katie."

"Yes, you are," Christina protested. "You *are* talented."

Melanie shook her head. "I love to ride. And I *love* ponying. But look at me: I'm a shrimp. I'll never be tall enough to be an event rider, like you, or to jump successfully, or whatever. I'll always just be a pony girl."

"You could be a jockey, like my mom," Christina said. "My mom would be so happy to have *someone* follow in her footsteps!"

Melanie smiled slightly. "I've thought of that. I might try it." She shook her head. "But after that bolt yesterday, I don't know."

"That's what I came to talk to you about," Christina said, grateful that Melanie had brought it up first. Was she still mad? She didn't sound mad. But Melanie was smart and subtle; sometimes it was impossible to tell what she was thinking.

"Listen, I'm sorry about that," Melanie said. "You were right; I shouldn't have tried the water jump."

"No, I'm sorry," Christina said. "I shouldn't have yelled at you. I know you were really scared."

"I was not scared," Melanie scoffed. "I just very strongly didn't want to fall off a horse going forty miles an hour."

The two girls looked at each other. Then they began to giggle.

"Okay, I was scared," Melanie admitted.

"I was, too," Christina said. "I thought you were a goner."

"It doesn't matter," Melanie said. "The point is, I'm not a good enough rider for Sterling. You need to find somebody more experienced than me."

"No, Melanie, you're fine with her. She was great on the flat with you, and as for the jumping, we'll just stick to the little stuff. You'll be fine. Please keep riding her for me," Christina pleaded. "Please? I want to ride in the event so badly. How can I, if you don't keep her in training for me?"

"After what happened yesterday, I don't really think I should, do you?" Melanie asked.

"She ran away with me too, remember?" Christina reminded her, holding up her cast. "That doesn't mean I shouldn't be riding her."

"Christina, look," Melanie said. "I'm not experienced enough to handle Sterling. You've got less than three weeks before the event. Sterling needs schooling, and you can't ride."

"I know all that," Christina said miserably. "What I don't understand is why I can't get anyone to help me."

"You can," Melanie said.

"I can't! I've tried everyone," Christina said disgustedly.

"You can," Melanie said again.

"Who?" Christina demanded. "You were my last hope, and now you're backing out!"

"Ask Cassidy to ride her," Melanie said quietly.

"WHAT?" CHRISTINA WAS ABSOLUTELY INCREDULOUS. HOW could Melanie suggest such a thing?

"Ask Cassidy Smith to ride Sterling for you," Melanie repeated.

"Melanie! You know what she's like. How can I ask her to ride my horse after what she did?" Christina demanded. "And I didn't even get a chance to tell you what she did today—when I went to turn out Sterling, she was riding her!"

"I know," Melanie said. "I heard you and Aunt Ashleigh talking about it."

"And you know about her going to the movies with Dylan. And I'll tell you something else." Christina suddenly remembered something from the first day she'd seen Cassidy. "Remember when you guys all came over to watch while I was having my lesson on Monday?"

"Yeah?"

"You remember how Cassidy started being really friendly to Dylan, and then she got him to go up to the barn with her?"

"I remember," Melanie said.

"Well, just as I was coming around to jump the liverpool, Cassidy and Dylan came back to the arena, and I saw them holding hands!" Christina said indignantly. "That's why I wasn't paying attention when I started to jump the liverpool." After delivering the news, she waited for Melanie to sympathize.

"You actually saw them holding hands?" Melanie asked incredulously. "How come none of the rest of us saw it, and we were right beside them?"

Christina thought back. "Well, I'm not one hundred percent sure, I guess," she admitted, "but it *looked* like they were. . . ." Her voice trailed off. Melanie was giving her one of her famous unwavering stares. It made her uncomfortable, and she had to look away.

Melanie sighed. "Chris, I don't know for sure what's going on between Cassidy and Dylan," she began. "But I know Cassidy's a really good rider. Obviously she's experienced enough to handle Sterling even if she misbehaves. We saw that yesterday. I only got Sterling under control because of her reminding me to use the pulley rein. And if it hadn't been for Cassidy stepping out and catching Sterling, I'd probably still be cantering around that ring!" Melanie said. "That was a gutsy move," she added, sounding full of admiration.

Christina looked at the drawing of Sterling Melanie had given her, and thought of the event. She wanted to ride in it more than anything. But the only way that was going to happen was if Cassidy kept Sterling in training. The thought of Cassidy riding Sterling gave her a strange feeling. It was almost the same feeling she got when she thought of Cassidy and Dylan going to the movies together, or holding hands.

"I just don't see how you really have a choice," Melanie said.

"I guess you're right," Christina said slowly. "But how do I ask her to ride Sterling after I was so mean to her?"

Melanie shrugged. "You'll figure it out." She turned around and opened her sketchbook to a clean page.

Christina sat on Melanie's bed for a moment. Then she got up and went to get the cordless phone from her parents' bedroom. She took it into her own room, dialed information, and asked for the Smiths' phone number. Then she sat on her bed and stared at the phone, trying to work up the courage to call Cassidy.

Christina was nervous as she finally made the call and heard the voice on the other end answer.

"Hello?"

Christina tried to speak, but only a strange little croak came out.

"Hello?"

Christina cleared her throat and managed to get out the words. "May I please speak to Cassidy?"

There was a pause. "This is she," Cassidy said.

"Um, this is Christina Reese."

"Oh. Hi," Cassidy said, sounding wary.

"Look, I called because . . ." Christina took a deep breath and jumped right in. "I wanted to say I'm sorry about how I acted today, when you were riding Sterling." As she spoke she pictured herself ranting at Cassidy and Mona that morning. When she thought how she must have sounded, Christina felt completely embarrassed. "I shouldn't have yelled at you like that."

She waited for a response, but Cassidy said nothing. She wondered if the girl was about to hang up on her. "I'm really sorry," she said again.

"It's okay," Cassidy said guardedly.

"Are you still mad at me?" Christina asked. "I mean, I wouldn't blame you if you were. I know I've been awful." She closed her eyes and waited for Cassidy to yell back at her, or hang up the phone.

"I'm not mad," Cassidy said. She sounded sincere.

"You're not?"

"No."

Christina opened her eyes. "Good," she said with relief.

"I understand how you felt," Cassidy said.

"I didn't know Mona asked my mom," Christina explained hurriedly. She was still ashamed of herself, and suddenly it seemed important that Cassidy not think badly of her.

"I know," Cassidy said. "I'd be just as upset if I thought somebody rode Rebound or Welly without my permission."

"Who's Welly?" Christina asked.

"Welly's my other horse, the hunter I was telling you guys about. Wellington is his name, but I call him Welly. Actually, his whole, registered name is Wadsworth Wellington III," Cassidy told her.

Christina laughed. "That's so cute!"

"But the horse show announcers never say it right, so I just show him as Wellington," Cassidy explained. She sighed. "I sure miss him. And my jumper, Rebound."

"I bet you do," Christina said.

"You know how it is," Cassidy said. "When you ride school horses, you don't miss them as much. But it's different when you have your own horse. You get so used to riding them every day that when you miss a day it seems like a week."

"I know exactly what you mean," Christina agreed.

"You must be going crazy not being able to ride," Cassidy said sympathetically.

"It's the worst," Christina said.

"My horses will be up here soon. I can hardly wait," Cassidy said.

Christina was surprised at how easy it was to talk to Cassidy. In spite of the thing with Dylan, she was starting to think that everyone had been right about Cassidy—maybe she really *was* nice.

"Cassidy?"

"Yeah?"

"There's something I need to ask you," Christina said.

"What?"

"My cousin Melanie—"

"Oh, is she okay?" Cassidy interrupted. "That bolt was really scary, wasn't it?"

"Yeah," Christina said, remembering with a shudder. "Listen, Melanie's not going to ride Sterling anymore. And so I was wondering . . . I know I was awful to you this morning, but would you consider taking over as Sterling's exercise rider until my wrist gets better? I get the big cast off in two weeks, and then I think I'll be able to ride her fine, but I need someone to work her for me until then. Would you do it?" She paused, expecting to hear Cassidy say that she'd love to do it.

"I'm sorry, but I can't," Cassidy said.

"Oh, that's— What did you say?" Christina asked, sure she had misunderstood.

"I said I can't," Cassidy repeated. "I'm sorry."

"But . . . why?" Christina asked.

"Well, tomorrow I'm taking care of Dakota for Dylan, and my mom says I have to spend the weekend helping unpack. We're still moving in, you know, and there's tons of work to do around here. I'm probably not going to be around the barn for several days."

"Oh," was all Christina could say.

"Sorry," Cassidy said again. "I hope you can get someone else to do it."

"Yeah," Christina said softly. "Well, thanks anyway."

"It's been nice talking to you," Cassidy said.

"Yeah, you too," Christina said. "Bye." She hung up the phone.

"What'd she say?" Melanie asked.

Christina glanced up. Melanie was standing in the doorway. "She can't," Christina told her.

"Is she mad at you?" Melanie asked.

Christina shook her head. "I don't think so. She just can't. They're still moving in, and she has to help her parents unpack and stuff. She says she's not going to be around the barn for a while."

"Oh," Melanie said. "Too bad."

Christina sighed. "Another event down the drain," she said glumly. "I have the perfect Event horse, only I'm never actually going to get to ride her in an event. It's hopeless!"

* * *

The next few days Christina had to turn Sterling out because there was no one to ride her. By the third day, Sterling looked puzzled. Christina led her into the paddock, being careful to turn the mare around to face her before she slipped off the halter. Usually as soon as she was free, Sterling would turn and gallop to the end of the paddock, her tail in the air. Then she'd stop, spin around, and gallop back toward Christina, ducking aside a few strides before she reached her. Then she'd trot several times around the paddock, her beautiful neck arched proudly as she threw her front legs forward in a perfect extended trot.

This time when Christina released her, she just stood there, looking at Christina as if to say, *Aren't you going to ride me? What's the deal?*

Christina stood beside her mare, admiring her sleek build and feeling guilty. "I'm sorry, Sterling," she told her. "But I just can't do anything until I get this cast off my arm."

Sterling sniffed at the cast suspiciously, as if she didn't like it any more than Christina did. She snorted noisily, showing displeasure at the smell of the plaster. "I know," Christina said, gently stroking the baby-soft down at the pink tip of Sterling's muzzle. "I don't like it, either."

She gave Sterling a last hug and backed away from her. "Go on," she told her. "Go run around. It's the only way you're going to get any exercise for a while."

She hung Sterling's halter and lead on a fencepost. Then she climbed awkwardly up the fence with her one arm and sat on the top rail to watch Sterling frolic. It was one of the things she'd always enjoyed the most.

But Sterling was still looking worriedly at her. "Go ahead," Christina said. "Go on and play. I'm okay."

Sterling shook her head, still looking at Christina. She didn't run to the end of the paddock, but walked up to Christina where she sat on the fence. The mare nuzzled Christina's legs, watching her face all the time with her beautiful dark eyes.

"You know something's wrong, don't you, girl?" Christina said softly. "It seems like we're never going to get to do an event together, doesn't it?" She pictured the big spruce tree that she and Sterling had jumped so many times together. She thought wistfully of all the long trots and canters she and Sterling had had, building up their endurance for the cross-country course. "All that hard work for nothing," she said sadly.

Christina sat for a long time on the fence. And the whole time she sat there, Sterling stood right beside her, just as if the horse knew how bad Christina was feeling and was showing her support in the only way she knew how.

After a while Christina climbed carefully down. "Well, if you're not going to run around, you may as well go back in your stall," she said. She slipped the blue nylon halter over Sterling's ears and clipped the throatlatch. Then she opened the gate and led Sterling through it.

Katie was in the barn. She had Seabreeze crosstied in the aisle while she tacked her. "Hi!" she said when she saw Christina.

"Hi," Christina said. "Can I get by?"

"Sure." Katie unclipped one of the crossties and stood guard beside Seabreeze to be sure she didn't kick at Sterling when she passed. Seabreeze didn't like other horses too close to her. She gave one annoyed switch of her tail as Christina led Sterling past her, but that was all.

"Oh, Christina, Melanie was looking for you," Katie said.

Christina led Sterling into the stall and turned her around so that she faced the door. Then she took off the halter. "Bye, pretty girl," she said wistfully. "I wish I could ride you." She had just closed the door of the stall when she heard her cousin's voice.

". . . to be around here somewhere," Melanie was saying to Cassidy as the two girls entered the barn. "There she is. Christina!" Melanie called.

"Hi," Christina said as she hung up the halter and lead line on the hook outside Sterling's stall.

Melanie had a gleam in her eye, and a smile lurked at the corners of her dainty mouth. Cassidy was smiling outright.

"What are you two looking at me like that for?" Christina said suspiciously.

"Because we have something to tell you that we think you're going to like," Melanie said mysteriously.

Cassidy and Melanie exchanged knowing looks.

"What?" Christina asked.

"Tell her," Cassidy said.

Curious, Katie left Seabreeze crosstied and came down the aisle. "What's going on?" she asked.

"Tell me what?" Christina asked again.

"It looks like you're going to ride in the event after all," Melanie said.

"How?" Christina asked. "I can't get on and ride her in a horse trial after two weeks of turnout."

"I'm going to train her for you," Cassidy said.

"But I thought you couldn't," Christina said. "You told me—"

"I know," Cassidy said. "But I'll find the time. I just didn't believe you really wanted me to ride her. But then Melanie told me your plan—that you get the big cast off right before the event, so you could ride again if somebody keeps training Sterling. She told me how badly you wanted to ride, and Dylan told me how you missed out on the last one, too. How could I not help you out?" Cassidy said with a smile.

"Really?" Christina could hardly believe what she was hearing.

Cassidy nodded.

"Well, that's great!" Christina said. "That's just fantastic! When can you start riding her?"

"How about now?" Cassidy offered.

"Did you hear that, Sterling?" Christina said, opening the stall door and going to her horse's side. She put her arms around the mare's neck and hugged her, envisioning galloping over the cross-country course at Foxwood. "The event is on!"

As if she understood, Sterling raised her head and whinnied happily. She seemed to be saying that she was looking forward to it as much as Christina.

# 10

CHRISTINA AND KATIE STOOD BESIDE THE FENCE AROUND the arena at Mona's, watching Cassidy ride Sterling. It was three days before the event at Foxwood, and so far Sterling had been a perfect angel. In fact, when Christina watched Cassidy ride the horse, it was hard to imagine that Sterling had ever misbehaved as badly as she had.

Cassidy had taken Sterling for long trots across the pastures to keep her conditioned. She had ridden through the dressage test until Sterling seemed to know it better than Christina and Cassidy. She had jumped Sterling over courses in the ring and over natural obstacles in the pasture. Cassidy had even gotten Sterling jumping the liverpool, though she'd had to use the crop every time.

At first Christina had been torn about whether

or not Cassidy should use a crop on Sterling. But she'd finally decided that it would be okay as long as she didn't hit her hard. When Cassidy rode Sterling to the water the first time, the horse had hesitated and looked as though she would run out, just as she had done with Melanie and Christina. But Cassidy had held the horse straight and given her a well-timed smack with the crop in her right hand. Sterling had tucked up her knees and jumped the liverpool with room to spare, cantering away on the other side with a snort and a toss of her head, as if she were just glad to get it over with.

Christina had to admit the horse seemed to accept the stick without overreacting when Cassidy used it. And so far she'd only used it at the liverpool.

Christina had watched Cassidy ride every time that she could, even jogging out into the pasture with Sterling and Cassidy. She reasoned that she needed to stay in shape as much as Sterling. The novice course at the event would be about a mile and a half long. Christina thought if she could run that far, she could definitely ride that far.

On Monday she'd gotten the big cast off, because the X rays showed that the small fracture in her wrist was nearly healed. Her arm had looked like it belonged to an alien, all pale and dirty and smeared with plaster. It took a few days before the stiffness wore off, but now her elbow felt fine. She exercised the arm whenever she had time, lifting a small weight or squeezing a soft rubber ball to keep her fingers strong.

The doctor had given her a light brace that fastened with Velcro, which she could remove when she showered or dressed. "Just be careful," he had warned her before Christina left his office. "Be sure you keep that brace on most of the time. You could still rebreak the wrist if you twist it or fall on it."

"I will," Christina promised. Standing at the fence rail, she squeezed her fingers closed, imagining how it would feel to hold Sterling's braided leather reins again. She had missed riding so much. She could hardly wait to get back in the saddle.

"Today's the day, right?" Katie said.

"Right," Christina said, smiling broadly. "Today I get to ride my horse again."

"How does it feel?" Katie asked, gesturing at Christina's wrist.

"A little weak, but pretty good," Christina said, testing her fingers by opening and closing them. "I just hope Sterling doesn't decide to run away with me again," she joked. "I might not be strong enough to stop her."

She had been kidding, but when she thought of it, her stomach churned in a way it hadn't done in the two weeks she'd been off Sterling. What if the mare did run away with her? What if she really wasn't strong enough to stop her? What if Sterling had forgotten her and thought she was some stranger riding her?

*Stop it,* Christina told herself sternly. *You're going to be just fine.*

Cassidy rode up to the rail. "Ready?" she asked.

Christina nodded.

"Sterling's ready, too," Cassidy told her. "She's missed you."

Christina opened the gate and went to the center of the ring. Cassidy had dismounted and was holding Sterling for her. "Want a leg up?" she asked.

Christina nodded. The butterflies were in her throat by now, so she couldn't speak. She faced the saddle and bent her left knee. Cassidy took hold of it.

"One, two, three," Cassidy counted, and on three Christina jumped and felt Cassidy boost her into the saddle.

Christina sat for a second, willing her pounding heart to slow down. Why was she so nervous? *This is your own horse, remember?* she scolded herself. *Now calm down.*

"I'm going to get Mona," Katie said.

Christina nodded. Ashleigh had agreed that Christina could start riding again only with Mona's supervision. She sat in the saddle while she waited for Mona and imagined herself trotting calmly around the arena.

"Are you okay?" Cassidy asked her.

Christina nodded. She still couldn't speak. She clenched her fingers to try to steady her shaking hands, and she pushed her heels down because even her leg muscles were trembling. How could she be feeling this nervous when all her life she'd felt more comfortable on the back of a horse than in her own bed?

"Well, it sure is nice to see you back in the saddle," Mona said.

But even Mona's familiar, encouraging voice didn't make Christina feel any better.

"Let's turn the key in the ignition and take her for a spin," Mona joked, as if Sterling were a new car.

Ordinarily Christina would have laughed. Instead she just gave Mona a worried look.

Mona always knew when to stop kidding. She came over to Christina's side. "What's the matter, Chris?" she asked kindly.

Christina looked at Mona. Then at Cassidy. Then at the liverpool down at the end of the arena. There seemed to be a huge weight on her chest that made it hard to breathe or speak. At last she got the words out. "I can't," she said.

Mona's forehead creased into a worried frown under the brim of her baseball cap. "What do you mean, you can't?" she asked quietly.

"I can't ride her," Christina whispered. "I—I'm too afraid." When she said it, the weight came off her chest, but the fear in her became overwhelming. All she knew was that she had to get off. Quickly she dismounted, and for the first time in all her years of riding she was glad to be getting off a horse, glad to feel the solid ground under her feet.

"Chris, talk to me," Mona said. "Are you feeling sick?"

Christina shook her head, but now that she was off Sterling's back she could speak. "I just don't think I'm ready to ride her," she said. Then she looked at Cassidy. "But I know Sterling's ready to go in the event. You've been doing such a great job with her. Would you please ride her in the event for me?" Christina asked.

Cassidy gasped in disbelief. "But she's your horse, Christina. It's her first event, and yours. You should be the one riding her."

Christina shook her head again. "I'm not ready," she said firmly. "You take her. Please?"

Cassidy looked uneasily at Mona.

"Christina, are you sure?" Mona asked. "This isn't because of the crop, is it?"

"No. I watched Cassidy school her. I understand about the crop. But I just know I'm not ready for this," Christina told them. She looked away, and her eyes found the liverpool. The cross-country course at Foxwood had a water ditch jump. Christina shivered a little, remembering how her attempt at the liverpool had led to her terrifying bolt around the arena. She could still feel the thud as she hit the dirt and the awful moments afterward, when she had had to gasp for breath. "I'm just not ready," she repeated in a dull whisper.

"Cassidy, do you want to go on and ride Sterling in the event?" Mona asked.

"I guess so," Cassidy said, looking at Christina for reassurance. "If that's what you really want."

Christina tore her gaze away from the liverpool and looked at Cassidy. She nodded. "That's what I want," she said firmly.

The morning of the event, Christina woke up before her alarm went off. She got out of bed and parted the curtain to look out the window. It was five o'clock. The sun wasn't up yet, though the sky was steadily lightening. A thick fog lay over everything, making it impossible for her to see farther than the backyard picket fence.

She let the curtain drop and went to her dresser. She took out a shirt and tossed it on the bed. Then she took something else out of the top drawer. It was a long, slender package wrapped in green tissue. She looked at it for a moment, then quickly pushed the drawer closed.

Christina pulled on jeans and her shirt, gathered her hair into a ponytail, and, taking the tissue-wrapped package, padded down the stairs in her stocking feet. She grabbed a piece of fruit from the bowl on the table and stuck it in the pocket of a jacket that was hanging on the back of a chair. Then she found her paddock boots by the kitchen door, stepped out onto the doorstep, and sat down to lace them up. When she looked up again, the sky was streaked with red in the east and dull gray clouds were heaped in the darkness to the west, threatening rain.

Christina stood up and tucked the green package under her arm with the lightweight jacket. It was too warm to wear it now, but she'd need something if it rained. Then she trudged down the path, passed through the backyard gate, and headed across the pasture for Mona's. It was eerie walking through the fog-shrouded pasture. Once she got turned around and had to go back and grope for the fence until she was certain she was going in the right direction. Mona's barn sat on a hilltop, though, and she spotted it easily as soon as she came a little way up the rise.

In the barn was an air of busy but quiet intensity as everyone did the last-minute jobs that always had to be done before a horse show. Matt was loading water buckets into the back of the green pickup truck. Dylan was loading tack into the front storage compartment of Mona's big green four-horse trailer. Katie was tying up the last of Seabreeze's braids. Cassidy was just coming out of the barn with a grooming kit. And Mona was leading Sterling out of the barn.

"Hi, guys," Christina said.

They all responded, but everybody was too busy to say much. Christina suddenly felt left out. This was the first time she had been to a horse show with Gardener Farm that she wouldn't be riding herself.

When the horses were loaded, Christina climbed into the cramped rear seat of the pickup with the other kids. It was just a five-minute ride down the road to Foxwood Acres, and nobody said much on the way. Dylan was too sleepy to talk and just kept yawning hugely. Katie, who could usually always find something to chatter about, was uncharacteristically silent. Cassidy seemed wide awake but appeared to be thinking furiously about something. Christina was anxiously watching the sky. The sun had risen but quickly been covered by the mass of clouds moving in from the west. The air had a thick, humid feel, and it seemed much too still. Christina hoped the rain would hold off. Sterling hated the rain.

When they arrived at Foxwood Acres it was nearly six o'clock. Sure enough, a light drizzle had begun to drift from the overcast sky, covering everything with tiny drops. Dylan's brown hair looked like it was draped with cobwebs. Sterling's dark mane looked the same after she'd been unloaded for just a few minutes.

"Matt, take the buckets and start filling them with water," Mona directed. "Cassidy, take Sterling and lead her around the grounds. You can show her the dressage ring and the buildings, but stay away from the cross-country course."

"Why?" Christina asked. "Wouldn't it be a good idea to show her the course?"

"It might seem like a good idea," Mona said, "but if you show her the course, she'll be disqualified."

"Oh, yeah," Christina said. "I forgot."

"The riders get to walk the course," Mona explained. "But the horses are just supposed to jump whatever they're faced with."

Mona kept on giving quiet orders, getting everyone organized. Over the course of two days, the more experienced riders would have to perform in a dressage test, a rigorous endurance test where they trotted and cantered for miles, a cross-country course, and a show-jumping course. The novice riders would perform only on the first day. That was called a horse trial, Christina knew, and it was designed to serve as a sort of warm-up for the more demanding two- and three-day events the less experienced riders and horses would one day be ready to tackle.

The dressage tests would be first. Then the riders would start on the cross-country course. Before they jumped, the riders would go over the course on foot, fence by fence, so they could plan how to best ride the distances and the approaches to the fences. When they were actually jumping the course, there would be a judge at each fence who would record the rider's number and whether there where any faults: knockdowns, refusals, or falls.

"Come on, let's go take a look at the course," Dylan said when Cassidy come back with Sterling.

"Christina, can you take her for me?" Cassidy asked.

Christina took the reins and held Sterling. The thick mist had coated Sterling's long eyelashes with little beads of water, and she kept blinking.

"Don't worry, Sterling," Christina told her. "You won't even notice the mist when you're out there jumping. I hope," she added under her breath.

Mona went with Cassidy, Katie, and Dylan to walk the course, so Christina had to be content with studying the course diagram. "Are you getting this, Sterling?" she asked, because the horse seemed to be looking at the diagram with as much interest as Christina.

She soon had it memorized. Twelve fences were arranged over a mile and a half of pasture in a course that eventually looped around back to the start. It began with a low brush pile and ended with a small stone wall with a rail over it. There were other types of obstacles, mostly natural, all solid but with a rail or sections at the top that would come down, preventing injuries in case a horse accidentally hit the jump with a leg.

Christina could see the brush pile that marked the start of the course. The fences were all numbered, black on white circles for novices, and flagged to help the riders remember which way to jump them. "Red right, white left," Mona had drilled into Christina in her weeks of training with Foster and Sterling. "If you jump it from the wrong direction, you're eliminated." Now Christina closed her eyes and imagined riding over the course, testing whether she was still nervous. She felt fine when she imagined jumping the brush pile, but when she thought of the water ditch, she felt the butterflies stir, and she quickly opened her eyes, glad that Cassidy was riding in her place.

"Good morning, ladies and gentlemen," the announcer said over the loudspeaker, "and welcome to the Foxwood Acres Horse Trials. Coffee and breakfast is available at the concession stand over on the south side of the parking area. We'll be starting up at seven o'clock in the dressage arena, so will the novice riders please get ready? Thank you."

Christina went and stood by the dressage arena, where she would have a good view of the riders as they performed their tests.

A moment later Cassidy came down leading Sterling, her mane done up neatly in thirty-five perfect black braids. She looked gorgeous. Cassidy was wearing a navy blue riding jacket and had somehow managed to keep her beige breeches completely spotless in spite of the soggy weather. Dylan was already up on Dakota. Katie sat on Seabreeze nearby. When she looked at her former teammates, Christina almost felt like crying again. She bit her lip and took a few deep breaths until she was sure she could trust her voice. Then she went over to Cassidy to wish her luck. "You look so beautiful," Christina said to Sterling, stroking her neck wistfully.

"She does," Cassidy said. "She's ready, too. She's just been walking around looking calmly at everything. I thought she might be nervous, but she's acting like a pro."

Christina noticed that Cassidy was still holding her number in her hand. "Want me to hook your number on for you?" Christina offered.

"No thanks," Cassidy said. "I'm not going to wear it."

"What do you mean?" Christina asked uneasily.

"I'm not going to ride. You are," Cassidy said.

"What do you mean?" Christina said again, this time with panic in her voice. "I can't ride. You have to take her."

Cassidy shook her head. "You *can* ride," she said. "This is Sterling's first horse trial. And you should be the one riding her, not me. Mona and Katie and Dylan and I all discussed this already. You have to be the one to ride her, Christina."

"But I can't," Christina protested, feeling the ominous flutter in her stomach.

"Yes, you can," Cassidy said. Her voice was warm, and her green eyes held Christina's with calm assurance. "I know you can," she said firmly. "I know how you feel. Once I had a bad fall. I broke my leg. I fell off a thousand times before that, and it never bothered me, but after that time, whenever I thought about riding, I felt like I'd throw up."

"That's what I feel like, exactly," Christina said.

"I know," Cassidy said. "I avoided riding for the longest time. I kept telling my instructor and my parents that it bothered my leg too much and I needed more time. But really I was just scared to death. One day my trainer finally told me, 'That's enough. You either get on and ride, or we sell your horse and you take up tennis.' I thought he was being mean. But I got on. And soon I was trotting around. Then cantering. Then jumping. And pretty soon the butterflies just went away. Yours will, too," Cassidy said. "You have to get on, though. I know how scared you are, but if you don't do it today, you'll keep finding excuses. And then pretty soon you'll be taking up tennis."

Christina listened carefully. She thought about every word Cassidy was saying. "I'm not very good at tennis," she whispered.

"Neither was I," Cassidy said, laughing. "I belong on a horse. And so do you. This horse," she said, indicating Sterling. "So get ready to ride."

"COME ON, CHRISTINA. YOU CAN DO IT," DYLAN SAID.

"Cassidy's right," Katie agreed. "You should ride."

"But look at me," Christina said. "I don't have my show clothes. I can't go into my dressage test wearing jeans and paddock boots."

"You can wear mine," Cassidy said. "I'm only a little bit taller than you. What size breeches do you wear?"

"Twenty-four long," Christina said.

"Same as me," Cassidy said. "Come on, let's get you dressed."

Christina looked over to where Mona was standing and talking with another trainer. Mona glanced at her and gave her a reassuring smile. So they had planned this whole thing together. Christina could hardly believe it.

"Hey, wait," Christina said, grabbing Cassidy's elbow. "We can't change riders this late, can we? Isn't there some kind of rule about that?"

Cassidy shook her head. "If I'd gotten on Sterling today to school her, then only I could ride her. But I didn't," she said. "I just led her around."

"Thanks," Christina said. But her heart began to pound all over again when she thought about riding Sterling.

They went into the horse trailer and closed the door. "Private dressing rooms," Cassidy joked. "What will they think of next?"

"Maids to clean them?" Christina said, carefully stepping over a pile of manure to get to a clean spot where she could change. They both laughed and quickly began swapping clothes. Everything was a perfect fit except the boots. Cassidy's feet were a half size smaller than Christina's.

"They'll be all right," Christina said, though her toes were getting pinched.

"They'll have to be," Cassidy said. "Turn around," she ordered her. Christina obeyed and felt Cassidy hooking her number on the back of her collar.

There was a knock on the trailer door. "Girls?" Mona said. "Come on."

"Let's go," Christina said.

"Wait," Cassidy said. "Your hair." Quickly she took the hair net off her own head and expertly tucked Christina's ponytail into it.

"Hurry," Christina said.

"Christina, you're up in four," Mona said.

Christina knew that meant that four riders had to ride their test, and then it would be her turn. But she had to be up and ready before then. Cassidy handed Christina her helmet. Christina put it on, careful not to untuck her hair. Then she turned to Cassidy. "How do I look?" she asked.

"Like you're ready to ride," Cassidy said. "Let's go." The two girls hurried out of the trailer and followed Mona down the hill.

From the time she mounted up, Christina seemed to become numb. Her legs felt like they belonged to someone else, and she kept looking down at them to be sure her feet were still in the stirrups. The only thing she could actually feel were the butterflies. They hovered at about chest level as long as she concentrated on the dressage test she was about to ride, but swelled into her throat if she thought ahead to the cross-country course.

She was thankful that Dylan went before her. She watched him ride Dakota expertly through the test and give the halt and salute at the end. She even forgot her anxiety for a moment when she noticed how handsome Dylan looked in his show clothes.

"Just completing the test was number one-twenty-five, Dakota, ridden by Dylan Becker," the announcer said. "Now entering the arena, number one-twenty-seven, Sterling Dream, ridden by—" He paused.

Christina knew he would be reading the change of rider on the list in front of him. "Christina Reese."

Suddenly Christina realized she was supposed to be entering the arena. She shortened her reins and somehow managed to get Sterling into the ring. On her way in, she passed Dylan coming out.

"Go get 'em," he said, smiling warmly at her.

All during her time in the ring Christina was conscious of the directives of the test sounding through her head in sequence, like a recording playing in her mind: *A, enter working trot sitting. X, halt, salute, proceed working trot sitting. C, track left. H, working trot rising. E, circle left twenty meters . . .* But she didn't know *how* she made it through the test, because she couldn't feel her body at all. It was as though her head were attached to someone else's body. When she came out of the ring, Cassidy was waiting for her with a huge smile.

"Christina, that was really good," Cassidy said. "I bet you're going to get great marks for that test."

"You looked terrific out there," Katie said, reaching out to squeeze Christina's hand as she passed her on her way into the arena.

"That was the best you and Sterling have ever ridden the test," Mona commented. "How did that feel?"

*Feel?* Christina hadn't felt anything. She was still numb from head to toe. She was convinced that Sterling had simply executed the test herself, because she'd done it so many times. She watched Katie and Seabreeze's test, all the while wondering how she was going to jump a cross-country course without being able to feel her arms and legs.

There was some time between her test and the start of the cross-country course, but Christina couldn't have said how long it was. She just knew that somehow she was in the start box, waiting to go. She had traded Cassidy's show jacket for a polo shirt she'd brought along, but she had no recollection of actually changing shirts. When she tried to guess how much time had passed since the dressage test, it seemed like five minutes, and at the same time it was like a hundred years.

The one moment she did remember was unwrapping the green tissue package she'd brought from home. In it was a long black jumping bat, with a rectangular flap of leather at the end. The handle was rubber, to ensure a good grip if it got wet, and had a knob at the end to keep it from slipping through the rider's hand.

The bat had been a Christmas gift to Christina from her parents, before she ever had Sterling. She had always connected it with the Event horse she'd hoped to own someday, and had kept it tucked in its original green tissue, thinking she would use it when she was finally riding cross-country on the horse of her dreams.

Of course, she'd never used the bat with Sterling.

She'd brought it along that morning, intending to give it to Cassidy as a good-luck gift.

But now she sat in the start box, her fingers squeezed around the handle of the bat. One person was allowed to be in the start box if the horse or rider needed it, and Mona stood beside her, telling her in a quiet, encouraging way about the course. Katie was walking Seabreeze around nearby.

Dylan had come back not long before. Dakota had been both sweaty and wet from the mist as he galloped up the hill and cleared the last wall jump before riding to the finish. Dylan had told Christina that Dakota had stumbled in a mud puddle after one of the jumps and nearly gone down. If the horse had fallen, they would have been eliminated, but he'd managed to stay on his feet. Dylan had fallen off, however, incurring a penalty and costing him time while he struggled to mount up again, his feet slippery with mud. Christina's heart was in her throat as she pictured something similar happening to her.

"How am I ever going to do this?" Christina asked, the fear causing her voice to sound wooden.

"Just ride," Mona told her. "Just like you did in the dressage test. Don't think about it. Just ride."

"But I didn't even walk the course!" Christina said, beginning to panic again.

"No, you didn't, but you *do* know the course," Mona said. "You've told it to me a hundred times, and Dylan talked you through it after his round. You know the fences and the landscape. You know how much time you have. And you know the trouble spots to watch out for—the oxer at fence six, where Dakota almost fell, is getting slippery on the landing side. Jump it to the left, where the footing is better. Everyone is going too fast and ending up with speed faults. Take your time. Trot a few fences. Fence nine is the water ditch. It's not wide, and it's flanked by trees, so it's inviting to jump. When you're about three strides away, hold your bat back behind your leg, like this." Mona demonstrated. "Then you'll be ready in case she tries to stop or run out."

Cassidy stood just outside the enclosure. "I schooled her over the liverpool a bunch of times," she reminded Christina. "She doesn't like the water, so she hesitates, but she'll jump it. When you're almost at the takeoff, just give her a little tap, and she'll pop right over," Cassidy said reassuringly. "Won't you, girl?" She reached over the fence and gave Sterling an affectionate rub. The mare tossed her head. She had been surprisingly calm all through the day despite Christina's own nervousness.

"Okay, you're about ready to start," Mona said. "I'm out of here." She gave Sterling a final pat and backed out of the start box.

Christina turned and looked at Mona with complete terror. Cassidy's lips were moving, telling her something reassuring, but Christina's heart was pounding so loudly that she couldn't hear anything else. Her legs were quaking. How was she going to ride like this? How would she ever be able to jump a course like this?

But then the start signal sounded, and she couldn't think about it anymore. She had to ride.

Christina trotted toward the first fence. The little brush pile, flagged with red and white and numbered with a small round sign, seemed like a huge tangle of thorns and weeds growing tentacles that groped for her and Sterling as she trotted closer and closer to it. *But you didn't even walk the course!* Christina told herself. *How am I supposed to jump a course I've never seen before?*

Then she reminded herself that Sterling had never seen the course, either. They would face each fence together. And then somehow they were over the brush and past it, trotting down a gentle grassy slope toward fence number two.

It was as if the fear had disappeared and the only thing in Christina's head at that moment was the course. And as she found fence two and cleared it, then looked around for fence three and spotted it thirty yards away, she realized that she knew the course just as surely as if she'd walked it. She had studied the diagram so hard it was engraved in her head, as clearly as if she were still standing in front of it.

As she made it over fence three she saw the terrain

unfolding in front of her. Comparing it with the picture in her head, she knew that fence four, a log pile, lay just on the other side of the hill before her.

She let Sterling canter up the hill, and sure enough, there was the log pile. She trotted it because she was jumping slightly downhill, then cantered on into a cluster of pine trees. She pictured fence five in her head: a coop painted green and flanked by standards. Sure enough, it appeared before her at the end of the trail through the trees. Then she was over it and on to the next fence, the oxer.

Suddenly the butterflies flew up wildly again, and Christina could hardly breathe as she cantered toward the oxer. The ground was marshy there, and sucked at Sterling's feet. Sterling pinned her ears, and Christina knew she hated the muck, hated the wet and the rain that was starting to come down harder.

She remembered Dylan's warning about the slippery landing side of the oxer and Mona's instructions. Carefully she aimed for the left side of the jump and saw the fence judge step back to give her plenty of room.

On the other side of the jump a large puddle was spreading rapidly. She could see skid marks in the mud where Dakota had slipped. Then she was clearing the jump, landing in the grass to the left of the puddle.

Fences seven and eight were small verticals with brush underneath them, set on an easy bending line six or seven strides apart. Sterling jumped the first, then turned and cantered to the second in seven strides, clearing it gracefully.

Christina turned to look for the next fence, and suddenly her mind was a blank. What was the next fence?

She looked around frantically and didn't see it. The course diagram had vanished from her mind as if it had never been there. She couldn't remember it where it was or what it looked like. Sterling's canter slowed as Christina hesitated. "Oh, no," she said aloud.

Before her were two stands of willow trees, about fifteen feet apart. Suddenly she heard Mona's voice, as surely as if she were standing next to her: *Fence nine is the water ditch. It's not wide, and it's flanked by trees, so it's inviting to jump.* Then Christina saw the number nine on its circular card and the red and white flags. "Found it!" she said with relief, and the rest of the course popped back into her head, too.

But her relief only lasted a second. As soon as she recognized the fence, Christina suddenly felt almost blind with fear. She couldn't think, she couldn't feel—she could only watch the ditch come closer and closer to Sterling's cantering legs and picture with calm certainty the runout that would result in her falling off.

But then Mona's words came into her head again, and because she didn't know what else to do, she obeyed them. *Hold your bat behind your leg,* Mona had said. Christina did it. Sterling cantered on, splashing through the growing puddles as the rain came down harder and harder.

She was almost at the takeoff, and she could see into the ditch now. It was usually a friendly little creek, fed by a tiny spring. But the rain had swollen it and deepened it, and the water rushed along in muddy swirls. She felt Sterling hesitate, felt her gather herself to stop and duck to the right, and a vision of the liverpool at Mona's popped into Christina's head.

But then she remembered the bat in her hand and heard Cassidy telling her, *When you're almost at the takeoff, just give her a little tap with it.*

Christina had a vision of Sterling abused in her stall by her old groom. How could she hit her? *Just give her a little tap with it.* She remembered how she'd hit Sterling in front of the other liverpool, too hard because she was angry, and sent the horse lunging into the water. She was holding the bat right behind her leg. What if Sterling freaked out again and stumbled into the water? *Just give her a little tap with it.* She was at the takeoff for the water ditch, and Sterling was about to stop, Christina knew; the horse actually raised her front legs, which meant she was about to spin around and run away from the hated water.

Christina had never been so terrified, ever. *Just give her a little tap with it,* Cassidy's voice said again, and somehow Christina did it: She tapped Sterling with the bat, and instead of wheeling away, Sterling gracefully cleared the water ditch, giving her hindquarters an extra kick back at the water as if to say, *Take that!*

And in the five minutes or a hundred years after that, Christina found fences ten and eleven and galloped up the gentle slope to the little wall that was fence twelve. She rode past the finish cones and looked around, lost for a moment, until she spotted Mona, beaming and coming to give her a hug.

"You did it! Christina, you did it!" Mona said. "I am so proud of you!"

Suddenly Christina realized what she had done, and a happy smile broke though the mask of fear and tension she had worn all through the day. "I did, didn't I?" she said in happy amazement. "I rode through my first horse trial."

She slid to the ground and realized that she could feel her legs again, and her arms, and her wrist, which was throbbing a little from the exertion. But she was glad to feel it; pain was wonderful compared to numbness. The only thing she couldn't feel anymore were the butterflies.

She spotted Melanie and Kevin waving at her.

"What are you two doing here?" she asked.

"Cassidy called us and told us you were riding," Melanie explained. "We couldn't miss that!"

Cassidy was hugging her then, and Dylan was congratulating her, and they both wanted to know how she thought she'd done.

"Where's Katie?" Christina asked.

"She should be coming in soon. She started about five minutes after you," Mona said.

"Did you have any penalties?" Dylan asked.

Christina tried to remember but wasn't sure.

"What happened at the water?" Cassidy wanted to know.

Christina looked at Cassidy solemnly. "I did exactly what you said. I held my bat back, and when I was almost at the takeoff, she hesitated."

"And what happened?" Cassidy asked.

"I gave her a little tap," Christina told her.

"And did she stop?" Dylan asked.

Christina shook her head slowly. "No. She popped right over it. Can you believe it?"

"I knew she would!" Cassidy said.

Just then Katie came back. She had made it through the course with just one knockdown. Christina, Dylan, and Katie compared notes for a while as they waited for their scores. As soon as the scores from the cross-country course reached the office, they were combined with the dressage scores. Then they would be posted on a big board.

When everyone had ridden and all the results were in, Dylan and Katie went with Cassidy to check the standings. Christina said she didn't want to know her score. She was just happy that she had ridden.

She was sitting with Melanie and Kevin, holding

Sterling's lead line and letting her graze, when Dylan, Cassidy, and Katie came back.

"How'd you do?" Christina asked Dylan.

"I came in seventh in the individual," he said.

"That's great!" Christina said. "And are the team scores posted yet?"

"Not yet," Dylan said. "But Christina, you've got to come over to the board with us."

"Come on," Cassidy said, taking her arm. "You've got to see this."

Mystified, Christina gave Sterling to Melanie and Katie and went with Dylan and Cassidy to the board where the scores were posted. "You guys, I told you I don't care about my score," Christina reminded them. "I'm just happy I did it."

Then she realized that Dylan and Cassidy were pointing to her number on the scoreboard.

"So?" Christina said. "I don't know what all those numbers mean."

Kevin and Melanie had been too curious to stay behind. They walked over to the scoreboard, leading Sterling.

"What's the deal?" Melanie asked.

Kevin was scanning the postings. "Christina!" he exclaimed. "You've got the winning score!"

Startled, Christina started comparing the scores. Hers was the best. At the same time the announcer read off the standings. "In first place, number one-twenty-seven, Sterling Dream, ridden by . . ."

Christina didn't even hear the rest of the announcement. "We won?" she said in amazement. "Sterling won?"

Katie hugged her, Melanie high-fived her, and Cassidy congratulated her. Christina threw her arms around her horse's neck and thanked her. Then they all listened anxiously as the team scores were announced.

". . . at our novice team trials. In first place, the team from Gardener Farm," the announcer declared.

Katie, Dylan, and Christina all cheered and high-fived each other. Mona was beaming. "You guys are wonderful," she said.

Then Christina heard someone standing very close to her say, "I knew you could do it." It was Dylan, and before Christina could answer, he planted a firm kiss on her cheek.

Christina felt her face turn completely red, but to her relief, Dylan didn't seem to notice. He was happily discussing the course with Kevin.

Christina leaned her head against Sterling, closed her eyes for an instant, and thought about Dylan's kiss. She realized the butterflies had all come rushing back—but this time they were fluttering with joy!

**Allison Estes** grew up in Oxford, Mississippi. She first sat on a horse when she was four years old, got a pony when she was ten, and has been riding horses ever since. Ms. Estes lives in New York City and works as a trainer at Claremont Riding Academy. She plays on four softball teams and, between games, has written over a dozen other books for young readers.

created by Joanna Campbell

# Read all the books in the Thoroughbred series and experience the thrill of riding and racing, along with Ashleigh Griffen, Samantha McLean, Cindy McLean, and their beloved horses.

MAIL TO: HarperCollins Publishers,
P.O. Box 588 Dunmore, PA 18512-0588

**Visa & MasterCard holders —call 1-800-331-3761**

**Yes, please send me the books I have checked:**

| | Title | Number | Price |
|---|---|---|---|
| ❑ | **Ashleigh's Hope** | 106395-9 | $3.99 U.S./ $4.99 Can. |
| ❑ #1 | **A Horse Called Wonder** | 106120-4 | $3.99 U.S./ $4.99 Can. |
| ❑ #2 | **Wonder's Promise** | 106085-2 | $3.99 U.S./ $4.99 Can. |
| ❑ #3 | **Wonder's First Race** | 106082-8 | $3.99 U.S./ $4.99 Can. |
| ❑ #4 | **Wonder's Victory** | 106083-6 | $3.99 U.S./ $4.99 Can. |
| ❑ #5 | **Ashleigh's Dream** | 106737-7 | $3.99 U.S./ $4.99 Can. |
| ❑ #6 | **Wonder's Yearling** | 106747-4 | $3.99 U.S./ $4.99 Can. |
| ❑ #7 | **Samantha's Pride** | 106163-8 | $3.99 U.S./ $4.99 Can. |
| ❑ #8 | **Sierra's Steeplechase** | 106164-6 | $3.99 U.S./ $4.99 Can. |
| ❑ #9 | **Pride's Challenge** | 106207-3 | $3.99 U.S./ $4.99 Can. |
| ❑ #10 | **Pride's Last Race** | 106765-2 | $3.99 U.S./ $4.99 Can. |
| ❑ #11 | **Wonder's Sister** | 106250-2 | $3.99 U.S./ $4.99 Can. |
| ❑ #12 | **Shining's Orphan** | 106281-2 | $3.99 U.S./ $4.99 Can. |
| ❑ #13 | **Cindy's Runaway Colt** | 106303-7 | $3.99 U.S./ $4.99 Can. |
| ❑ #14 | **Cindy's Glory** | 106325-8 | $3.99 U.S./ $4.99 Can. |
| ❑ #15 | **Glory's Triumph** | 106277-4 | $3.99 U.S./ $4.99 Can. |
| ❑ #16 | **Glory in Danger** | 106396-7 | $3.99 U.S./ $4.99 Can. |
| ❑ #17 | **Ashleigh's Farewell** | 106397-5 | $3.99 U.S./ $4.99 Can. |
| ❑ #18 | **Glory's Rival** | 106398-3 | $3.99 U.S./ $4.99 Can. |
| ❑ #19 | **Cindy's Heartbreak** | 106489-0 | $3.99 U.S./ $4.99 Can. |
| ❑ #20 | **Champion's Spirit** | 106490-4 | $3.99 U.S./ $4.99 Can. |
| ❑ #21 | **Wonder's Champion** | 106491-2 | $3.99 U.S./ $4.99 Can. |
| ❑ #22 | **Arabian Challenge** | 106492-0 | $3.99 U.S./ $4.99 Can. |
| ❑ | **Ashleigh's Christmas Miracle** | 106249-9 Super Edition | $3.99 U.S./ $4.99 Can. |
| ❑ | **Ashleigh's Diary** | 106292-8 Super Edition | $3.99 U.S./ $4.99 Can. |
| ❑ | **Samantha's Journey** | 106494-7 Super Edition | $4.50 U.S./ $5.50 Can. |

Name ______________________________

Address ______________________________

City ____________________ State ______ Zip ________

SUBTOTAL . . . . . . . . . .$________

POSTAGE & HANDLING .$________

SALES TAX . . . . . . . . . .$________
(Add applicable sales tax)

TOTAL . . . . . . . . . . . . .$________

Order 4 or more titles and postage & handling is **FREE!** For orders of fewer than 4 books, please include $2.00 postage & handling. Allow up to 6 weeks for delivery. Remit in U.S. funds. Do not send cash. Valid in U.S. & Canada. Prices subject to change. H19311